I0524947

The Day I Saw

The Hummingbird

A Novel

PAULETTE MAHURIN

Copyright © 2017 by Paulette Mahurin

All rights reserved. No part of this book may be reproduced in any form or by any means, electronic or mechanical, including photocopying, recording, or by any information storage and retrieval system, without permission in writing from the author. Exception is given in the case of brief quotations embodied in critical articles and reviews. This is a work of fiction. Names, characters, places, and incidents either are the product of the author's imagination or are used fictitiously.

ISBN: 978-0-9993116-2-2

Published by Early Girl Enterprises, LLC

Printed in the United States of America

Dedicated to BC

Other Books by Paulette Mahurin

THE PERSECUTION OF MILDRED
DUNLAP

HIS NAME WAS BEN

TO LIVE OUT LOUD

THE SEVEN YEAR DRESS

Slavery is the next thing to hell.

Harriet Tubman

Foreword

In many southern states, educating slaves to read or write was illegal. A universal fear was that black literacy could undo the foundations of slavery whereby slaves relied on their masters. The majority of southern whites believed that literacy could ultimately lead to a rebellion, with educated slaves demanding rights equal to white people. For example, in South Carolina, a 1740 law levied oppressive fines on offenders who educated slaves. In Virginia, an 1819 law regarding assemblages or schools to teach slaves to read and write stated, "any justice of a county…may issue his warrant, directed to any sworn officer or officers, authorizing him or them to enter the house or houses where such unlawful assemblages may be, for the purpose of apprehending or dispersing such slaves, and to inflict corporal punishment on the offender or offenders, at the discretion of any justice of the peace, not exceeding twenty lashes." In Louisiana, an 1830 law stated, "that all persons who shall teach, or permit or cause to be taught, any slave in this State, to read or write, shall, upon conviction thereof, before any court of competent jurisdiction, be imprisoned, not less than one month nor more than twelve months." Nonetheless, at the risk of punishment to offenders, slaves continued to be clandestinely educated by whites and other slaves themselves. It was with great delicacy that I incorporated the element of educating slaves into this story and, in particular, with the protagonist and narrator of the story. Therefore, the narration contains the voice of a very fortunate, educated, escaped slave.

Many of the scenes depicted were adapted from historical notes, letters, and other documentation from slaves who lived to tell their stories. Language considered racist by today's standards was commonplace in the time period during which the story takes place and was included in certain dialogue to lend authenticity to some fictional characters. Fictitious people, places, events, and geographical settings have been added to enhance the story line, for example where Booker T. Washington gave a lecture honoring Harriet Tubman. Lastly, aside from the use of the real names of Harriet Tubman, Booker T.

The Day I Saw the Hummingbird

Washington, Julius Rosenwald, and John Rankin, real people are portrayed with pseudonyms.

The Day I Saw the Hummingbird

Prologue

SUMMER 1914

My skin flushed with excitement as I ambled along the long stretch of walkway leading up to a large brick building on the campus of the Tuskegee Normal and Industrial Institute. Oh, what a sight it was, with what looked like acres of surrounding lawns and oak, pine, and cottonwood trees brimming with singing mockingbirds and robins. I got a good feeling when I saw a reddish-orange breasted robin eating a worm, its belly full and puffed out, and then fly free to look for another. *You're free, little bird, just like me, ole Oscar Mercer.* Although the sense of freedom was in my bones, the pain that memories brought—never a moment away from rebirth—pulsed with my beating heart.

The Day I Saw the Hummingbird

The huge building was nothing like the stations that kept me safe many years ago: the Underground Railroad safe houses. But it did remind me of the sugarcane plantation I toiled at with its typical southern facade of four majestic white columns housing the entrance. Just the mere reminder of what I'd left behind so many years ago gave me pause. Years of freedom had not erased the nervousness I still felt lifting my head around white people in the South. Now flanked by some white folk (who were coming to meet Mr. Rosenwald, president of Sears & Roebuck who was a trustee of the Tuskegee Normal and Industrial Institute and sponsoring today's lecture), even though other Negroes were present, I couldn't shake the distrust that lived in my body. All the kindness and compassion I'd experienced from those who helped to free me never replaced the sour taste left from the torture and injustice at the hands of the mean foreman that defined my childhood. *Lower your head Oscar,* I could still hear my mama scream. *Don't be looking where your eyes don't belong.* Later at night when away from the sugarcane field, my mama, Catherine Mercer, her big brown eyes wide as the moon and her nostrils flaring, would whisper in my ear. *Your curiosity is gonna get us killed.* Her sweet breath pounded on my cheek as the intensity of her tone increased. *Look at your feet.* And when I gave her a blank look (as I often did), she shook and scolded me to *listen while I be talking to you, Oscar.* She would then shove a loose strand of her jet-black hair stuck in perspiration off her forehead. I loved her mannerisms, they were very telling when she was nervous about something.

Memories surged through me as I recalled the years it took to comprehend why my mama was so stern yet so loving. With time came answers, horrible answers, and with that came understanding and respectful love for the woman who gave me life. She wasn't the only woman who gave me life. Yes, she birthed me, loved me, and did more than right by me. But there was this other woman who indirectly saved my life through her work helping lots of folks. Even though I never met her, today I'd be celebrating Harriet Tubman. Booker T. Washington was giving a talk honoring her. And I was attending. This was one of the many lectures he was doing concerning educating Negroes and paying tribute to those who helped free us.

The ghosts of the past mixed with excitement as I relaxed my shoulders into a slow, deep breath and felt the warmth of the Alabama sun soaking into my back. The last of the sun's rays shining over the roof moved into the shadow of the entryway as I made my way up the steps to the building. Aside from a few coughs, the sound of feet shuffling, and muffled whispers, it was very quiet—not like the streets I just traveled that were filled with the echoes of horses' hooves clip-clopping, carriages' wheels creaking, loud laughter, and all that goes with life's carrying on. No, here among the fragrance of perfume on the finely dressed women and wisps of men's cologne, ascending the stairway of the building, there was an undercurrent of stillness, respectful quietude. It was the kind of absence of noise—a scarcity of idle chatter—that made my body feel good, in harmonious balance with natural things like those singing mockingbirds and robins I heard earlier. It's how I used to feel when the sun went down and the moon rose in the sky during sleepless nights in the slave quarters. Back then, the clittering of crickets took my attention off the bad things, the things I didn't want to think about. Today those thoughts flitted in and out of my mind as I made my way toward the lecture hall.

My gaze on the steps, I noticed all the new-appearing shoes and felt proud at how clean and shiny mine were. Not like all the years ago when I wore a pair of hand-me-down shoes that were too big for my feet. They caused blisters that made me limp, slowing my work. I could still feel the beatings from the whip that burned on my back because I didn't move fast enough. How many nights had I gone to sleep wishing my feet would grow enough to feel comfortable in those shoes? I remember the day Mama handed me a thick pair of socks. I never knew where they came from, but it made all the difference. It was a wish come true, my prayer for protection. Maybe because it felt too foreign to consider freedom, I prayed for what I might be able to have: an article of clothing, enough food in my belly, proper sleep to sustain me another day, and even a song to sing to lift my spirits without fear of a lashing.

As I entered the building, people moved in closer proximity, and the combination of body heat and the warm, humid day made me sweat. Feeling the moisture bubbling on my forehead, I took a clean, white, neatly folded handkerchief from the back pocket of my new pants and wiped my forehead. I gazed around to see if anybody noticed. *Wipe that sweat off your face, boy! You gonna look guilty.* The memory of my mama whispering to me as I stood next to her in the line of pickers who were being tongue-lashed by the ugly foreman played in my mind. He was mad because our crop yield was low that day. *Lazy niggers,* he screamed. Back then, I didn't have a cloth to wipe myself; I used my sweaty forearm to clear away the stream of perspiration.

A friendly woman saying, "Excuse me," as she bumped into me, interrupted my ponderings. It felt mighty fine that a southern white woman had the decency to treat me like a full human being. And today that's exactly how I felt: complete.

But it wasn't always like that.

Chapter One

1852

I was born in Louisiana on a large sugarcane plantation outside of New Orleans. My papa, Mack Mercer, came from a long line of Congo indentured servants. They worked in a system of unfree labor (employed against their will by threat of destitution, violence, detention, and other intimidations). They were bound by a contract to work for an employer for a set period of time. Once they satisfied their contract, they were granted freedom and (occasionally) a plot of land. The growth in the Atlantic slave trade changed many of these domestic-indentured servants' relationships to slaveholder-chattel slavery. It was then that the working poor Africans became captives and were shipped outside of the Congo (and other African regions) to America. This is how my papa's family landed in Louisiana on a sugarcane plantation and where he met my mama, Catherine. Her lineage is unknown to me.

I've been told they took an instant fancy to each other. When I was old enough, I'd listen to stories about how after a long, laborious workday out in the sun—in the rare spare moments at night in their slave quarters—they got to know each other. Women and men were bunked separately in small, one-room wooden shacks. Mattresses were strewn on floors, and there were brick fireplaces to cook meals and keep them warm on the cold winter nights. My papa would sneak over to the cabin my mama shared with five other women and tap on the outside wall. Mama used to laugh when she told me it was a fairly regular occurrence. "The women giggled and nudged, 'Go on Cat, your man calling.' One of them girls hear your papa calling me *his kitten*. She stopped calling me Catherine. Nicknamed me Cat. It done stuck and spread faster than lard in a hot pan."

When word of their affection got back to the plantation owner, Mr. Thomas Coleson, he shared the news with his wife, Margaret. Since it was widely believed that married men were less likely to run away because they had wives and families, the Colesons encouraged my parents to wed. The Colesons also favored my parents' marriage for religious reasons and wanted my mama to have children, many of them. Rumors spread that a woman who bore more than ten children was granted her freedom. My mama told me once that many of the slave men were reluctant to marry women from the same plantation, as they couldn't bear to see them ill-treated. "Not your papa," she'd say to me "he want to wed. He hope someday we see freedom." And so the union between Mack and Cat Mercer—my parents— occurred. I never found out how old they were at the time. But they must've been a couple of years shy of twenty.

Two years later in early 1852, my mama became pregnant with me. Little did they know that I was to be their only child. My mama would not go on to be ordained her freedom through multiple childbirths. Or by any other means.

Mama's one and only pregnancy was a rough one. She told me that she had awful nausea and vomiting. It started in the morning and lasted until well into the day when her struggles with retching quieted. As the months moved along, not sufficiently hydrated and weak from long hours in the fields, she failed to gain adequate weight to keep up her strength. And as the wintery cold warmed into spring, it was Mrs. Coleson who demanded my mama rest, take herbs and calming teas to gain an appetite, and be fed food that was easy on the belly that she would be able to keep down. That was the part of the story I liked the best, when she had been shown kindness.

Thomas Coleson, at his wife Margaret's insistence, informed Joseph Prescott, the foreman, to keep my mama off the field. That was the start of the conflict between Prescott and Papa. That man Prescott did not like being told what to do and hated having to cater to one of the slaves. My mama told me that he had the eyes of a rabid dog ready to kill at the slightest provocation. To Prescott, the slightest provocation was someone asking for water or a break to pee. My mama's pregnancy was ample provoking for that awful man, but he didn't take his vengeance out on Mama. Instead, it was my poor papa who felt his wrath.

The story of how my papa suffered from Prescott's cruelty became lore passed along at night in the slave quarters for years. I heard it many times before I escaped. There was a particular day when Papa had been up all night with Mama. She had bad belly cramps. He rubbed her feet and back, got her cold compresses, and sat her up to give her sips of fluid until the sun rose and he had to get back out in the fields. When he arrived on the field at sunrise, Prescott was waiting.

"Move your slow ass, nigger!" He screamed at Papa who was bent over picking sugarcane.

When Papa craned his neck to look up at Prescott, a hard fist came down on his right cheek, knocking him flat to the ground.

"Get up you lazy—" He coughed out the words with spittle flying and his eyes glaring. His straight-blond hair, parted down the middle, flew over his forehead, and he swatted at it to clear it out of his eyes. With left eye twitching, Prescott repeated, "I said get up! And I ain't gonna to say it again, you lazy bastard!"

Papa, still dizzy and unable to gain his upright balance, fumbled.

Prescott stomped his boot to the ground. Dirt flew into Papa's face as he was attempting to stand.

Papa fell back to the ground.

Prescott went wild. He found a long, hard tree limb lying on the ground, picked it up and smashed it on my papa's right hand. His bones crunched and skin burst open instantly. As my papa went to grab hold of his hurt hand with his good one, Prescott hit him again, this time smashing the other hand. Broken bones protruded through two deformed hands by the time Prescott was finished with him.

That night, my parents got no sleep as friends in the living quarters tended to my papa. My mama was devastated. Every time she'd repeat this to me or was next to a friend telling the story, she cried. Oh, how I wished Mrs. Coleson knew of this abuse and would have asked her husband to stop it. But no one dared to say a word. Not a soul wanted to risk being Prescott's next victim. Knowing that punishment would come to those who talked or complained, no one did. To get under Prescott's skin (and we never knew what that might be) meant anything from a beating like Papa got to being attacked by his bulldog, Buddy. Or worse. If that wasn't bad enough, there was his crew: Smitty, R.J., and Jake Coulfield. They were no better. The slaves knew that Prescott and his crew weren't beating us just to teach us lessons; they were doing it because they liked it. We didn't stand a chance. Sadly and through no fault of his own, my papa got the worst of it.

The next day when Papa went to work with his hands bandaged, Prescott scoffed, "Claws," referring to the clubbed appearance of Papa's hands. They looked like bear claws. There was no letting up on his wickedness.

"Don't be thinking I'm going easy on you." He loosened his grip on Buddy's leash and threatened, "You slow son of a bitch, you better keep up your workload!"

My papa took a breath and held his tongue.

"Did you hear me, boy?"

My papa nodded.

"I can't hear you, Claws!" Prescott gave his dog a nod to start growling. "You better speak up or your ugly face will get a beating."

"Yes, sir," Papa said with eyes cast downward.

Prescott tightened his hold on Buddy and moved on. Out of the corner of his eye, my papa saw him take a flask out of his back pocket and guzzle the liquid. Papa could tell that flask was filled with whiskey. He said he smelled it on Prescott's breath during all that yelling.

The days continued like that with Prescott riding my poor, broken Papa like a wild bull. No whipping was too great, no abuse out-of-bounds. Name-calling, dirt-throwing, and inciting Buddy to pee on him were bits of the story that spread at night in the cabins. *He done nothing to deserve such treatment* was whispered in the slave quarters. *Mack don't do no back-talking, not even a look or whisper. Why Prescott so mean to him?*

It went on like this for months. My mama continued to attempt to sooth him in their quiet nighttime together. Papa did his best to carry on, divert his eyes, and refuse to speak or even show any expression that would reveal his true feelings. His anger, grief, powerlessness, fear, and hopelessness were hidden deep inside. Even to my mama. But she saw what he tried to keep hidden in his silent head nods and predictable obedience. I feel choked up thinking about the look on her face when she told me this.

It was a mixed blessing when Mama reached term with me because it distracted Papa's attention. On October 3, 1852, after long, hard months for my papa, I was born. "Oscar," Mama held me in her arms and smiled at my papa. "He be named Oscar, after my father," she said. Mama told me that Papa smiled plenty that night as he held me in his arms.

My name never took with the nasty foreman who called me "Clawson" when he first saw me. Mama decided to take me out to the field with her instead of leaving me behind with a babysitter. That gave her a break three times a day to breastfeed me. That awful man used to drink his liquor and harass the breastfeeding women in the field. And there were nights when he had too much of the sauce. He would stagger around and grab a slave out of the women's cabin to have his way with her.

My mama, a pretty woman with shoulder-length jet-black hair pulled back into a knot, had a kind face with soft brown eyes, full lips, and straight nose. She was pained when Prescott hovered over her while she was feeding me. "Clawson," he spat. "He got a big breast to feed from. Yes, indeed." Prescott looked down on Mama. "He gonna make a big fat field slave."

My papa, five-foot-eleven inches in his bare feet, was a strong, muscular man. He had a rounded face with short-cropped, jet-black hair and a small, angular nose. Mama told me, "He always had them soft hazel eyes. But they wasn't always so sad." She liked remembering when his heart-shaped cracked lips had the "sweetest smile." I remembered the time her attention drifted away before she returned her gaze to me and said, "Sure wish we'd see more of that smile of his."

Maybe it was in the very first air that I ever breathed in, but from the very beginning, I got a sense of turmoil all around me. A feeling that, to this day, knots my gut. And I hated that there was nothing either of them could do about it.

The Day I Saw the Hummingbird

Chapter Two

Even though I wasn't old enough to fully understand, my mama confided in me. I think she needed to. She would repeat things as I grew older and began to comprehend better. Like the time my parents worked until ten at night. She told me this story so many times that I could picture it like I was watching it happen to someone else's baby. Mama left me in the small cabin with Sammy, a ten-year-old slave who had the job of watching the younger children so their mamas could go to work. He later moved on to fieldwork. I never found out what happened to his parents, but rumor had it they both died from inhumane treatment out in the fields.

Sammy carried me to Mama for breastfeeding then brought me back to the small, stuffy room where we spent the day. There were five babies in total. I had been coughing the night before, and Mama worried that being out with me all day would be too much. I was four-months-old, and she felt comfortable leaving me. By the time my parents arrived back after their work, they were exhausted. And I was fussing with fever.

Papa took hold of me from Sammy and once back in our cabin said to Mama, "He pretty warm, Cat."

Feeling my forehead and cheek with the back of her hand, she moved toward a bucket of water kept in the cabin for washing. "Strip his clothes off." She washed me down and blew on the back of my neck and entire body to cool me. When my panting slowed, she looked up to my papa. "He be all right now. He just fine, our strong baby boy."

Papa put a hand to Mama's sweaty back, feeling the moist cotton dress that was stuck to her skin. "This ain't no life for a person, let lone a baby. I wish—"

Mama shook her head and responded, "Mack, we need be fixed on where we is, not where we wish we be going. Ain't no use in wishing and living in dreams. That surely cause us suffering." And with a smile that I'm sure warmed his anxious heart, she continued, "We got each other. Our boy all right. We got food and this here," she looked to the ceiling, "roof over our head." When she shared past stories, she used to love to fill in all the details: how he looked, how she felt, what she noticed. She needed to talk, and I liked to listen.

The Day I Saw the Hummingbird

I could feel the emotions as Mama described things that happened. Like the night my papa moved his deformed hands behind his back and lowered his head in what looked like shame he was trying to hide. Mama told me that she often wondered if he felt that somehow the beatings were his fault. How awful that must have been for him, my poor tortured papa. She also said she saw his misplaced guilt. "I done tell your papa all that happened, ain't none of it his fault. He took too much to heart. But you can't control how others are gonna be," she whispered to me.

She was a wise woman, my mama.

"But," she said, "when I done tell him it wasn't his fault, it didn't help. Oh, that look he wore on his face—a big bundle of pain—hurt my breast to see. He tried hard to hide it, putting a silly-looking smile on his face. But I knew...No fooling your mama." Her words came in a slow, serious tone. "That night, he toss and turn. Made my body feel prickly, like there was danger coming."

But, she told me, nothing dangerous happened right away.

The next morning, like every other morning, my folks were up before sunrise, had porridge, removed their sleeping gowns and got dressed. My papa wore his dirty, beige, heavy cotton pants, cotton shirt, socks and shoes, while Mama was in her long cotton dress and head-wrap. That was their warm weather and summer dress. When the seasons changed and it became colder, they were given additional clothing to wear or material to make their own. As for me, I guess I had hand-me-down baby clothes.

Dressed and ready for work, my parents (along with other slaves who lived in cabins near them) trudged out as the sun sat on the edge of the horizon. I continued to stay behind with Sammy and was brought to Mama for breastfeeding. My parents usually returned after dark, when the moon was high in the sky. Day in and day out, this was our life.

There wasn't much new to talk about and conversations pretty much remained the same, so when the chatting stopped, singing started outside on the small porch where neighbors gathered. There were rare occasional changes in the routine and talk. One night, my mama mentioned to Papa that she had seen the postal carrier arrive in a big hurry. Dust was flying and hooves were banging. Prescott being Prescott, he just had to leave his post to find out what was being delivered. That man had a powerful need to know everybody's business. She told me that my papa whispered that maybe someday they'd get on a horse and ride away.

"Wishing, wishing, wishing. Mack, you ain't never gonna stop."

"Cat," he half-smiled with a far-away look in his gentle eyes. "My sweet Catherine, you gonna see. I could be right 'bout it."

Little did they know that while Papa was daydreaming about us riding away on horseback, a woman named Harriet was working alongside a group of fine men and women to help this fantasy become reality. It would be years until word of the Underground Railroad arrived at our doorstep.

My parents didn't have much in material possessions. But what they did have was love and the few occasions when they knew laughter. They'd get out on the porch to sing with their friends, too. Their voices had a strong beat full of the melody of faith. It was rare, but there were occasions when they sang during the day while working in the sugarcane field.

When Prescott was in a good mood, singing was allowed; so were limited breaks and a reasonable amount of time for lunch. There were even the special occasions (when crop yield quotas were met) that the slaves got to go home at sunset. And their Sunday half-day time-off was honored. But when Prescott's mood soured—when he drank too much or something got under his skin—the routines, rules, and measure of comfort they provided all disappeared. Those were the days of hell on earth for the field slaves.

I remember the time when I was two-years-old. I was giggling and toddling around the cabin with Sammy chasing after me. That day Mama came back early. I know it was early because the sun was still high in the sky and it was warm out. She picked me up and walked me the few steps to our little place, quiet all the while. When she sat me down, her voice cracked and she moaned, "Oscar, my baby."

I didn't have full comprehension of the words, but her tone was crystal clear. She was in pain. Bad emotional pain. I reached up for her, for a hug. She put her arms on my shoulders and looked me in the eyes, tears now streaming down. "Oh, my boy, how I gonna say this?" She was whispering.

Just then I heard loud footsteps.

Bang! Bang! Bang! Someone pounded on our door. It flew open.

A man screamed, "Get her back to work!"

The Day I Saw the Hummingbird

The next thing I remember is being grabbed from Mama and brought back to Sammy. I was slammed into his arms with a mean voice yelling, "Take him!"

Later that night, Mama returned from the field without Papa. I sensed something was terribly wrong. It made my arms itch and break out in hives. My rash got better, but Papa never did come back to the cabin. Ever.

The Day I Saw the Hummingbird

Chapter Three

Mama tossed and turned for hours, moaning and coughing, just saying, "Oh, Lord. Oh, Lord. Oh, Lord." Awake from either the sound of her distraught voice or the tension in the air (maybe both), I fussed and cried right along with her until she reached a dry, calloused hand over to my body and moved me closer. "Shh, now, Oscar." Then, she muttered a low-pitched gurgling, awful whine. Her cracked, downturned lips pressed on my cheek. Her hug was as weak as her voice. It felt as if the life had been drained from her.

I let loose a scream that sat her up straight. She undid my diaper to check if I had soiled it. When she found it was dry, she cried, "You feeling it too, ain't you, my boy?"

Neither of us slept that night. When Mama lit a candle to gently light the room the next morning, I saw her big, red, puffy eyes. Seeing Mama like that filled my little body with fear. My papa was gone, and now, by the looks of Mama, she'd be taken from me, too.

Even at my very young age, I could tell what happened just by being around Mama. I knew it was something bad. Awful. Mama's pain was a solid mass of sorrow, and it punched me straight in my belly when she whispered, "Papa's gone on to a new home for a while. He be treated right and good where he at." That was my first taste of what suffering felt like. It was like a powerful ache in every part of myself that no poultice nor rest nor fancy white doctor could cure. I came to believe that that ache was as much a part of me as my skin.

Even as a baby, Mama used to tell me that she knew I had a compassionate soul. She said she could tell by the way my eyes widened with disbelief when she told me stories about Papa and other injustices slaves had to endure. "Yes, my sweet baby boy, you do understand. Don't you?" In hindsight, I don't know if I was reacting to what she said or how she said it, the tone of her voice. As far back as I can remember, what my mother expressed, how she felt, seemed to emotionally settle into my body.

Years later, the slaves still talked about the horrible event. That's how I found out. It had been an especially hot day. Prescott carried a rawhide whip in one hand and a bottle of booze in the other. My mama, bent over picking sugarcane, lunged forward when Prescott grabbed hold of her backside. Laughing, he yelled, "Come on over here Smitty." When Smitty was behind Mama, Prescott raised the skirt of her dress. "Have yourself a grab of that big, fat, black rump."

The minute Papa caught sight of what was going on, he stopped working and ran to Mama's defense. Smitty smacked him across the cheek, throwing him off balance.

Prescott dropped his whip and grabbed a gun from his belt. He shot my papa smack dab in the middle of his forehead, sending blood and brain flying. Mama fell to the ground screaming, "Why? Oh, Lord! Why?"

"Get up!" Prescott commanded. A cold chill ran down me as I remember being told that he continued with disgust written all over his face when he said, "You want to be next. And then we'll go for that nigger boy of yours." Prescott, scratching his crotch, turned toward Smitty "Think that nigger baby would make good alligator bait?" he laughed.

"One way to find out," sneered Smitty.

Prescott turned to Mama, still stooped by Papa's lifeless body, her warm hand on his cheek. "Get that fat butt of yours moving!" he slurred.

Smitty stood by laughing.

That was the day Mama came to me early. She was on her lunch break. They wouldn't even let her have a few minutes of grieving before they dragged her back to work. My blood still boils just thinking about that horrible day. And if there is a God creating beauty and goodness, there must be a devil that filled Prescott with hatred and a heart of stone. I have no other way of explaining how human beings can be so wicked to one another.

* * *

I sure am grateful to my mama for not giving up on life and sticking around for me. That's the kind of big love she had for me. Months after Papa's death, Mama would lie in bed with me and whisper, "You my life, Oscar. I gonna do right by you. You my life."

My faith in my mama's strength was reinforced as the weeks moved into months and the months moved into years. By the time I was five, she was breathing easier. Even though she was mostly a quiet woman when she spoke, it was with a fiercer voice. "Lower your head and look down when them bosses around," she'd say. "But you keep them insides mighty." With her finger pointed at my heart, she'd continue, "That where strength is." Then she would smile and her eyes would light up, her voice soft. "You know who you is and you is a strong, good boy." Then the fire always came to her words when she'd say, "Don't you ever be acting like Mr. Prescott or his kind. You hear me?"

"Yes, Mama."

At night, with the others out on the porch and me perched on Mama's lap, a whispering moved among the good people; it was filled with a hushed excitement. I like to call it the sound of hope. It was surely the promise of freedom. With Mama's hand on my arm, I felt her warmth. Night by night, the murmurs continued, and the muted excitement grew.

"I hear tell of a Negro woman working to free our people. That right?" someone mumbled in Mama's earshot. She sat erect waiting for the reply. When a head nod came, Mama's mouth widened into the biggest smile she'd had since my papa left this earth.

"Them just tales. Don't be getting our hopes all up for a bunch of nonsense," lamented a slave named Pursey.

"It ain't no nonsense, Pursey," replied Mama's friend Albert. "My daughter, Macy, overhead something—"

Pursey interrupted. "Them house girls like to chatter," referring to the fact that Macy was a house slave.

"Wasn't our folk doing the talking. My girl overheard Mrs. Coleson say something." Albert went on to relay that Macy had walked in to serve a dinner party while the missus had just mentioned a Negro woman who was working with a group to help free slaves. "When she saw my girl, they done stopped talking." He smiled.

"Oh, Lord." Mama looked to the clouds floating by in the starlit sky as if in prayer. "I knew you was there."

The rumors continued until one day when they were validated. It happened when a deliveryman brought horse-feed hay to the plantation. The usual man who helped unload was gone, and a field worker was called upon to do the unloading. When the driver saw it was a field slave, he discretely nodded. In the barn where the hay was stored, the driver was able to very quietly let the slave-helper know that people were working to free slaves. He said he'd figure out a way to get word back to anyone who wanted to try to escape.

That night, the porch was buzzing with the news.

"That too dangerous," said Pursey.

"You wanna spend your days like a dog?" asked Albert. "Worse than a dog," he continued. "Least they let their animals rest and cool off."

"You right!" Someone else agreed a little too loudly.

"Shh, now settle down. We gotta be smart 'bout taking in this news," said Albert.

Holding onto me for dear life, Mama sat silently listening.

That was the beginning of the talk about the Underground Railroad involving a network of people: black and white folk working hard to help free slaves. That was the first I heard of the woman named Harriet.

The Day I Saw the Hummingbird

Chapter Four

As time moved on, no word was had from the deliveryman or anyone else. My sixth birthday was approaching. I was now working the fields alongside Mama. So was Sammy, who had been my babysitter. Another younger girl took over his baby watching duties. I was glad to have his company.

As far as Mama, the rejuvenation she felt from talk of freedom had subsided along with the others. The dullness her eyes that had shown after Papa died had returned. Pursey's perpetual drumming of "I told you it be nonsense" didn't help. Pounding it into our ears, he yammered on about what fools we all were to be entertaining that anyone would help free a slave. "No one gonna risk his hide to be helping us."

I'd go to sleep at night with the sounds from Pursey's mouth crowing in my head. That didn't bother me as much as Mama's reaction to it, slumping shoulders and all. She'd tuck me in at night and, through a deep, sorrowful-sounding sigh, she tried to keep that promise of freedom alive. "It gonna happen, Oscar." Wiping tears from her eyes, she continued, "Don't you never stop believing the Lord be good and..." Then the tears would overwhelm her.

"Don't cry, Mama. Don't cry," I pleaded.

She brushed my cheek with her wet hand and kissed my forehead. "I love you, baby boy."

I felt that love. I think having me to love and protect was the only thing that kept her going. Especially during the days when Prescott had his crazy fits. That man drank like he was stranded on dry land. And he encouraged his crew—Smitty, Jake Coulfield, and R.J.—to follow his lead. I never understood why he couldn't just drink the booze alone and leave the others to tend to their work. But, no, he had to get them all riled up and going wild. That's when big trouble started. It didn't take me long to learn to slouch, do my work, mind my business, and keep my mouth quiet. All I could do was hope he wouldn't send a stinging whip across my back like he had before. Or the backs of anyone in striking distance for no reason other than for his amusement.

The Day I Saw the Hummingbird

The earlier time when I was whipped was a day I was laboring in the fields and dust settled in my nose. I sneezed. That sneeze made him mad.

"Get back to work!" he slurred.

Unfortunately, I sneezed again.

Prescott threw his booze down, grabbed his whip, and slashed my back. Once. Twice. Three times. It was the fourth strike that ripped my shirt and drew blood. The wounds burned into my young flesh, but what scared me more than the pain was what Mama would do seeing her little boy needlessly and ruthlessly whipped by the drunken Prescott. I hoped she continued on working with her head down like she taught me to do. She did. Mama knew to mind her business.

That night back in our cabin, Mama rubbed my back with soothing salve. Each gentle stroke of her hand brought all the tears I had held back earlier as Prescott whipped me. "There you be," said Mama as she turned me to face her. "You gonna heal just fine." The words Mama didn't speak that night were painfully expressed in her heartbroken eyes. I felt that pain deep in my chest, like a hand ripping my heart out. I was too young to fully understand Mama's restraint. And I was still too immature to fully grasp all the meanness that came from

Prescott and his men. To this day, it still puzzles me how people can hurt someone like that. It took me years of feeling a lot of hatred, anger, resentment, and murderous rage to ultimately come to understand that acting on those feelings does no good. Restraint, a valuable lesson from Mama, was what I learned. It kept me alive. And that's what Mama wanted most for me.

The painful memory of my first whipping faded as Prescott lumbered toward us. I caught a glimpse of his bloodshot eyes beaming a hatred that chilled my bones. Someone was in for it. Mama had told me many times that Pursey's mouth was going to get him into big trouble. Sadly, she was right. Prescott came at him like a wild hog ready to kill, violently shaking his whip in one hand and holding a long branding iron in the other. Paying attention (but not wanting to look directly at what was happening), I kept my gaze to the ground and continued with my work.

Prescott screamed, "Get up, you lazy nigger!"

Dirt flew into my nose and mouth as Pursey scrambled to stand on his shaking legs. Acid rose into my stomach. I feared I may lose my breakfast. I took a hard swallow to clear the mud stuck in my throat.

"Smitty!" Prescott called over to Smitty, who was standing with Coufield and R.J. a few feet away. "Get over here."

Smitty approached, swaying as he tried to strut. His laugh sounded hard. I smelled the booze on the spit that spew from him when he said, "Yes, boss."

"Take this," Prescott handed the iron to Smitty. "Heat it up and get right back here."

The smell of liquor still lingering in the air was replaced by a foul odor. Pursey must have gone in his pants. It made my chest tighten.

Pursey moaned, "What'd I do?"

"Shut your mouth!" Prescott commanded. "That big black mouth of yours. That's your problem."

Next thing I heard was what sounded like a boot kicking Pursey, a thud on the ground and a moan from wounded Pursey.

"You stupid idiot. I know 'bout the talk." Another kick. "You think someone's gonna to come and free you!"

I was startled that Prescott knew our secret. We had been so careful to refrain from discussing it except in the private moments out on the porch at night. *Was someone listening in and had told on us?* No wonder Mama rarely said anything.

When Smitty returned with the hot iron, all hell broke loose.

"Get over here," Prescott yelled to Coulfield and R.J.

"This is gonna be good," Smitty snickered.

"Hold him down!"

The more Pursey resisted, the angrier their voices became. But they were laughing, too. I've tried to forget the sight and sound of Pursey's cruel attackers enjoying themselves. I can't. They weren't behaving like humans.

When they were finished with him, R.J. who was usually the quiet one, smacked his lips and said, "Get back to work."

Pursey crawled back to the plot of earth where the sugarcane was in need of picking. Favoring his scorched left arm, he did his best to keep at it. That night, no one went out on the porch.

Before bedtime, in the darkness of our little cabin, behind the safety of the walls where our time was easier, I asked my mama, "How come that man do that to—"

"Hush now, baby. Don't be asking what no one can answer. Some folk just have meanness in them."

She hugged me close and sang a gentle lullaby in my ear. Her breath warmed the coldness that afternoon had left me with. When her voice cracked, I knew she was crying right along with me.

"Mama," I reached my arms around her neck. "I scared."

"I know, baby. I know." Her response was a sweet breeze. Thinking we were done for the night, she surprised me when she said. "There ain't many people you can trust with your words. Always be watching what comes out of your mouth. Once you say something, once something is said, there ain't no getting it back."

She was referring to whoever snitched on us by telling Prescott about our freedom talk. She was trying hard to teach me a lesson that would prove to be very important in my future survival, but the words didn't impact me as much as her actions. My mama tended to practice what she preached.

"No one?" I echoed. And then I thought of seeing Mama talking a lot with Albert. His soft, kindly face sat well on his large-framed body.

"You be lucky if you find a friend in life that can hold his tongue. Don't mean folk be bad. Just human nature to talk 'bout things."

"You don't talk much, do you, Mama?"

"Not much, honey. Outside of your papa, only one person here…"

In that silent moment when I knew she was at a loss, I filled in what I felt she was about to say. "Like Albert?"

"My, you is a wise little one. Don't miss much, do you?" My hand on her cheek, I felt her lips turn into a smile. "Yes. Albert knows to keep to himself. Knows to not talk 'bout what other folks say."

"I like him, Mama. And I like Macy, but how come she hardly ever comes around at night?" I was referring to the fact that Albert's daughter only came to see him on the half-day Sunday when we had time off. I thought of Macy's sweet, inviting face. One that was approachable. One I felt I could rely on. For some reason, Macy's general pleasantness made it easier to believe what she said. I never did find out what happened to Albert's wife. Whenever the subject came up, he became quiet, and Mama would inevitably change the conversation.

"Macy work in the big house. Has to spend her nights over there." Mama turned to look out the small window. And seeing the large, bright moon high in the sky, she said, "Time to put chatter aside and rest our souls."

The Day I Saw the Hummingbird

As I drifted off to sleep, I thought of Pursey and the big, red, blistery welts the branding iron left on his skin. I wasn't asleep long when my full bladder woke me up. Just shy of wetting my sleeping outfit, I got up, went outside and emptied myself in a bush short of the outhouse. As I turned to go back to my bed and my sleeping mama, I had to go again. The rest of the night played out that way. Back on my mattress, I thought about the freedom talks. I looked out at the brightness of the moon and wondered if at this very moment the lit-up night was helping someone escape.

The Day I Saw the Hummingbird

Chapter Five

Exhausted from all my sleep interruptions during the night, I was not ready to wake up at the usual before-sunrise time the next morning. I kept my eyes shut until I heard what sounded like a vole. Those Louisiana voles look similar to mice with a little stouter body, a more rounded head, and hairy tail. I had no idea it wasn't a mouse until years later when someone showed me a picture of one in a book. Oh, they made my skin crawl. So did spiders and beetles. I didn't like all those creepy crawling critters that inhabited our living space. I never knew if one would be inside when we returned home and Mama had to get them out. I was never much help on that account, but that particular fear of mine that sent me into a squirming, wiggling, shaking dance did make her laugh. And oh, how we welcomed the laughter.

Waiting and listening to see if the patter was inside or outside, I hugged the blanket to my chest. When the noise faded, I figured it was safe to get out of bed. Trying to avoid anything creeping around on the floor, I slowly tiptoed to my socks and shoes. I put them on with haste and shook my body to get rid of a crawling sensation spreading up my arms and legs.

Trudging out to the sugarcane fields, Mama nodded to an overgrown section we'd been working in. She mentioned, "That there crop be ready for picking." It was at the end of a ten-month cycle. The season's growth could go anywhere from nine to twenty-four months. I always liked when it wasn't the first planting, which meant we could cut the cane at the lower stem and leave the rest to grow more crop. Crouching down close to the ground and sawing through the entire shoot was hard enough. But the first seeding required the backbreaking job of digging up the whole plant and reseeding the earth. If the earth wasn't irrigated, that dirt was hard to move. After the first seeding, this cycle could be repeated around four times before replanting was needed. That meant that, during those times, we were potentially spared from digging new ditches if the old ones had dried up.

Even though some things were relatively easier than others, the hard work never ceased. When the sugarcane was picked and the fieldwork was done, Mr. Coleson had his slaves tend to the livestock, plant crops for the kitchen, or do odd jobs like fixing fences. He kept us toiling all year round. Through rain, sun, or air too thick to breathe, we plodded on in wet or dry fields, laboring from sunrise until after sundown on most days. The exception was the half-day off on Sundays.

Mama told me she heard from Albert that Macy overhead the Colesons talking about our workload. Mr. Coleson wanted to keep productivity up so we'd all have something to do with our time. Mrs. Coleson responded that perhaps we could have some time off, maybe even have someone come over and teach us to read and write. Apparently, Mr. Coleson put his foot down and yelled at her that educating slaves was illegal. The missus didn't care. Can you imagine that? The wife of a plantation owner in Louisiana advocating for the welfare of slaves? Without ever seeing her, I liked that woman. So did Macy. That conversation helped me understand why Macy didn't want to leave the big house.

I also learned later from Mama about another conversation Macy had with Albert about Mrs. Coleson not being able to have children. Macy mentioned that once Mrs. Coleson was pregnant, but the pregnancy was hard on her: she lost the baby. Something happened to her womb, and she couldn't get pregnant after that. Perhaps because Mrs. Coleson couldn't have her own children, she wanted to help others. For whatever reason, Macy said that the missus had a kind heart and gentle soul. That's why she liked working for her.

Maybe I'd have felt the same if I were in Macy's place. But I wasn't in her place. And at my age—approaching seven—I didn't like the life I was living, even though I knew nothing else. The promise of those freedom talks came back to my memory. They rang like a slow, methodical drum beat refrain in my heart and soul.

When I heard a swishing sound, my attention went back to my movement deeper into the growth of sugarcane. My shoes slushed on puddles of mud. There was plenty of water for the plants and then some. I resented that the crops were taken better care of than us. Many a night we had no water to bathe in. I hated going to bed covered in sweat and dirt. Mama did her best. She often reused filthy water. Although we weren't clean, rinsing off with anything wet that wasn't mud felt refreshing. "The sugarcane gets more and fresher water than we do!" I protested to her.

And as usual, she'd answer, "Shh now, we don't want complaining. That'll get you in big trouble."

The Day I Saw the Hummingbird

For all my resentment and disappointment, I knew she was right. *You gotta keep alive, son. Complaining ain't gonna to help you.* She repeated those words when things got tough. They kept me going. She'd often use those words referring back to a horrible day—a day that I'd never forget.

It all started out normal enough until Pursey stepped deep into a mud hole and twisted his leg. Calf-deep, he needed help getting out. That set Prescott off in a frenzy. He threw his drink to the ground and stormed over to Pursey, who was being helped by Albert and Sammy. "Let go of him and get back to work!"

Albert and Sammy moved on while Mama and I continued at our jobs.

Pursey made the terrible mistake of smacking his lips in earshot of Prescott. Whether he was in pain or just scared and forgot to keep quiet, we all knew he was done for the minute the sound came out of his mouth. He did, too. Bowing his head to his chest, he struggled to remove his hurt leg from the muddy mess.

When a growl came from Buddy and Prescott pulled out his gun, Pursey started to weep.

"Sorry boss. Clumsy accident. I be getting myself to work now," he pleaded as perspiration dripped from his forehead and mingled with pooling tears.

Prescott tightened the hold on Buddy's leash and demanded that Pursey stand up straight.

Pursey tried. He just couldn't straighten his leg.

I could see the panic in his eyes.

Prescott whacked him across the forehead with the butt of his gun.

That took care of the panic. Pursey, unconscious, went flying and landed face down in the mud. That big man Prescott stood there with his blue, bloodshot eyes bulging like they would pop from his angry face. He was a mean-looking sight with dark bags under his eyes and worn, leathery skin. For a foreman on such a bountiful plantation, he was a sloppy guy. His shirt was always flopping out from his belt, and his pants smelled like they need a good washing. "Get him out of here," he yelled.

A couple of other slaves assisted a now disoriented and groaning Pursey back to his cabin. They returned to work and told us he'd be fine. For the rest of that day, Prescott was in a foul mood bickering about the lost production because of "that stupid pig that had to be dragged off."

The Day I Saw the Hummingbird

I don't know why Prescott hated Pursey so much. Mama thought it was because of his constant complaining and squabbling, which must somehow have gotten back to Prescott. I learned later that Prescott used to come around at night and listen to our gatherings. He'd hide in the bushes. Sometimes he'd be alone and sometimes his dog would be with him; Buddy knew to be quiet when he gave the command. He had us all trained well. He'd drink, spy on us, and do much worse. No one knew when he would barge into a cabin to have his way with one of the women, pull an unsuspecting, fatigued slave from bed to beat on him for no reason or command Buddy to sic. Some evenings he'd bring his drunk flunkies to participate.

Prescott's hatred for Pursey came to a head later that night. There was an awful commotion outside our cabin that awakened Mama and me. We didn't dare go to look. But, we heard drunken screams from several voices. Prescott and Smitty were among them.

Scared and shaking, I went to Mama's bed for comfort.

"Lie here quiet," she whispered. "Anyone come in here, you keep still. Close them eyes of yours and act like you sleeping. You hear me?"

Understanding this was really serious, I nodded.

What followed were sounds I can still hear today.

A body being dragged.

Pounding thumps.

Prescott, Smitty and others were grunting and laughing about ropes and thick enough branches.

The rustling of leaves on a tree.

A loud moan from Pursey, "Noooo. Pleeeeze. I promise…"

Thud.

Creaking of tree branches.

That was the last thing Pursey ever uttered.

Chapter Six

The next morning, we cautiously left home. When we turned the corner to head to the field, there was poor Pursey—hanging dead from a tree with a rope around his neck. Mama tried to shield my face, but I broke loose and saw the worst sight my eyes had ever seen. I wish that wasn't my last image of Pursey: head bent, bulging neck with what looked like burn marks, and pants soiled from body waste. But I had to look. Something in my youthful soul wanted that sight etched into my mind to remind me of what hatred does. If ever I needed reminding how slaves should act, talk, or behave around men with power, all I needed to do was remember that vision of Pursey hanging on that tree. Before I turned away, I saw that disgusting, big, lumpy tattoo from the branding iron engraved on poor Pursey's left arm. My eyes were too blurry with tears to see anything more.

That day it was hard to shake the horrible sadness I felt. I knew Mama felt the same by the furrowed look of pain on her brow. She tried to be strong for me, but there was no amount of pretending that enabled her to hold her shoulders high. The heavy cloud of gloom hanging over us was crushing. Nowhere felt safe and there was nothing we could say or do to change that. Prescott had again invaded our spiritual refuge. It was a deeper emotional prison than toiling out in the fields as a slave.

The injustice of Pursey's death hit all of us pretty hard. And to make matters worse, we knew that it could have been any one of us. That madman Prescott had a terrible effect on our well-being, walking among us with that atrocious branding iron (or whip) in one hand and Buddy growling at the end of the leash in his other hand. The worst of it was the pleasure he seemed to get from preying on us. The more someone cowered, the greater the satisfaction showed in his countenance. Oh, I wish he were like Mrs. Coleson, who Macy said was good to her in her job. The missus even talked with her!

It didn't take long for me to realize that my daydreaming, wishing, and hoping for something better was useless. Mama used to tell me I had my papa's blood in my veins with how he'd continue to see things with hopeful possibility when she knew different. "Hope be a dangerous thing, son," she'd say to me.

She said that to me after the incident with Pursey. Turning my head from side to side, my confusion took hold of me and wouldn't let go. I understood that Prescott was dangerous. But hope? Dangerous? That made no sense.

Seeing my bewildered distraction, Mama tried to explain what she had meant. "You might not understand till you older. Maybe never."

In the quiet of our room that night, I urged, "Tell me."

"You get your hopes up, start expecting something, and you end up living in something may never happen. And when it don't, the disappointment takes your joy away. Best stay focused on what you have. What you doing. What the day brings and not stick your mind in a future that won't never happen."

"You can't say it won't never happen!" I protested.

"You just a dreamer. Like your papa. This ain't no black man's world we live in. You see us living like the white man?"

Mama made her point. She was definitely more grounded in reality. A very unjust reality. And when she saw my shoulders slump, she gave me a hug. Her love created the balance between my hating all the bad happenings about life and wishing for my life to be different than it was. Her love made me feel better.

As the days dragged on, we returned home each night to the constant reminder of Pursey: a mound of dirt. His grave, dug by Albert and Sammy, haunted us. We thought nothing would ever change to snap us out of our grieving until we got news from Macy. It was on a Sunday, our half-day off, when she came around to see her papa.

Albert, Macy, Mama, and me sat on our front porch. Others were busy with their own personal business: fishing for their meals; tending to small planting plots of fruits and vegetables; and one was mending cracks in the walls of his cabin to keep out the cold winter we were heading into. Mabel Johnston, an old woman with white hair, was out on her porch mending some clothes for the men in her family. She nodded over to us but didn't budge to come join in. Just as well because she had a way of shifting the conversation to focus on her, but we were in the mood for plantation gossip. And there was news to be heard.

Macy told us, "Mr. Coleson, he mighty mad 'bout Pursey's death. He talk with that mean," she lowered her tone, "you know who. Everything was denied..."

Albert and Mama understood what she was telling them from their headshakes and lip smacking. But I wasn't quite sure what she was referring to and made the mistake of saying a little too loudly, "Who? Who are you—"

Mama grabbed me by the arm and whispered, "Lower that mouth of yours! I'll explain later." And she did. But the version she gave to me was condensed. In simple words, Mama said that Mr. Coleson was not happy about losing a worker and he would be going shopping for a new one. That meant we'd have a new person arrive someday soon.

"What he be like?" I asked.

She shrugged her shoulders. "Dunno. Let's pray he be a good man like our friend, Albert."

The day that Mr. Coleson rode off in his carriage, he took two men with him, one of whom was Sammy. Sammy, who used to watch me when I was a baby, was now my closest friend besides Mama, Albert and Macy. He was nice-looking with slicked black hair and small facial features that danced around when he spoke. We worked closely together, and he often came around in the early evening to ask me if I wanted to throw rocks with him. That was our game. We'd put up an object several feet away and aim a stone at it. Sometimes when it was still light out, we'd see where it landed; when it turned dark, we knew by the pinging noise that it hit the mark. Later on, when Sammy and I spent a lot of time together, he mentioned he liked my mama. Although only around ten years older than him, she was like a mother to him. He didn't like to talk about what happened to his parents, and I didn't push it. Listening to him talk, I often wondered if Mama put him up to playing games with me to give me something to occupy my attention. Sammy came around asking to throw rocks just a couple weeks after Pursey died. I was still feeling too down in the dumps, so I said no. But when he kept coming around, Mama insisted I not neglect his feelings. "Go on out and spend time with him," she urged.

That friendship with Sammy was the start of a new beginning for me, but it would take me months to understand the magnitude of the role he was to play in my life. Mama used to refer to things as *the Lord's work.* I like to look back and feel it was Mama doing work on the Lord's behalf.

It wasn't until the new person arrived that I had an inkling of what all this Lord talk was about.

Chapter Seven

The year 1860 brought many changes. The Pony Express horseback riders became the most direct route of east-west communication (from St. Joseph, Missouri to Sacramento, California) before the telegraph was established. And Mister Abraham Lincoln was elected as the 16th President of the United States, the first Republican to hold that office.

Lincoln's election was followed by unrest. Starting with South Carolina's secession, eleven southern states would secede from the United States and form the Confederate States of America. What started as the South's attempt to maintain control over its economy—predominately based on agriculture and a plantation system that relied on slaves—resulted in fierce opposition to Lincoln's disapproval of the expansion of slavery and the government's rejection of declarations of secession. Thus began the Civil War.

Oppressive turmoil thick in the air weighed down on us while changes were also occurring on the Coleson Plantation. I was seven-years-old when Pursey's replacement, Kitch, arrived. At first, this new man only reminded me of the tragedy that befell my unfortunate friend. But that feeling didn't last long.

Arriving in the early evening just before we all got off work, Kitch and Sammy greeted us when we arrived back for the night. There was something about Kitch, who walked with high-reaching shoulders and his head erect, that I instantly took a liking to. He was a tall man, what I imagined must have been over six-feet tall without his shoes on. It strained my neck to look up to him. But when I did, there was his big smile, revealing several missing teeth. It reminded me of Mama insisting I wash my mouth to stop my teeth from yellowing. When I didn't listen, she'd hold up a piece of glass that reflected back color. "See, I told you they'd turn yellow. Best do what you can to keep them teeth in your mouth," she scolded.

Smacking my lips in one of my rare displays of protest, I shot a look back at Mama. "I don't like—"

She took hold of my face in both her hands. "Don't be sassing me now, Oscar. You gotta be good to that body of yours. It the only one you gonna get."

"I ain't sassing you, Mama. I don't like putting that big rag in my mouth to clean my teeth. Makes me feel like I gonna bring up my meal."

Mama's face lit into a smile. "Don't use so much material," she laughed. "Just a little piece and rub them teeth of yours clean as you can."

Feeling her laughter resonate in my body made me laugh back.

We fell into fits of giggles that went on for a good while. When it stopped, my lungs felt bigger, and my muscles lost a knot or two. With all the happenings around us, those moments of amusement helped us forget about Prescott and his men. They helped to keep us levelheaded.

Sammy clearing his throat brought me back to the present and Kitch's nearly toothless grin. They were involved in some communication about a little black book Kitch was holding in his scaly, rough hand. "This here's a Bible," he told Sammy, who had no clue what that meant. I could tell by the squinting, head-tilted look Sammy gave Kitch.

"It the book from the Lord."

There was that word again. The one Mama regularly used when upset or times when she'd look to the clouds as if wishing for something. Sometimes I'd swear she was conversing with Papa up in that big sky.

Mama, giving her full attention to Kitch, took in a deep relaxed breath.

"You know how to read that there book?" asked Sammy.

"Some of it," Kitch replied. "I'm still muddling through a lot of what I can't read or don't understand. But I can pronounce the letters into words."

"How'd you learn to do that?" I was curious and couldn't help joining their conversation. A strange and fascinating excitement crept under my skin. A new kind of hope that maybe all my daydreaming about what was possible—perhaps even freedom—wasn't just fanciful thinking.

"Had us a nice family at the last place I done worked. Some nights and sometimes on our few hours off on Sundays, the master's son come round and teach us to read. Even learned me and a couple of the others a little writing."

"Really!" I excitedly jumped up, hoping he'd offer to share some of his learning with us. Mama had said in her prayers that one day we may learn to read and write. I couldn't help wondering if there might be something to this praying business, now that Kitch showed up able to do both.

"Master's son, the one who done taught us, figured if we could read the Bible…"

Just then we heard what sounded like Buddy's barking. As the growling and woofing became louder, we froze. In a brief lull and without saying another word, we all went to our beds. I got on my mattress with my clothes still on and covered myself with a blanket. When Prescott and Buddy passed our place and headed for what sounded like the women's cabin, my nerves settled down a bit. Although he wasn't there for Mama and me, I still felt afraid for whoever he was after.

The Day I Saw the Hummingbird

Chapter Eight

The next day out in the field, Prescott went easy on us. It had me wondering if he was on good behavior because Mr. Coleson was still angry with him. Never mind the reason, it was a relief to do our day's work and get back while daylight was easing off. It gave Sammy and me time to get better acquainted with Kitch. And to our relief, there was not a repeat nighttime visit with Buddy's barking and growling. At least not yet there wasn't.

Jumping up and down, I squealed, "Can you learn me?"

Hearing the commotion, Mama came out from our place with a spoon in her hand that smelled of onion. "Hush now," she chided. She looked at Kitch, smiled, lowered her tone, and continued, "Don't wanna bring no trouble round here."

"Yes, ma'am," Kitch replied.

"Don't be calling me ma'am, Kitch," she puffed out her chest. "My name is Catherine. Friends call me Cat."

"Yes, Catherine," he said, looking from her face to the dripping spoon. He wiped a small drop of spittle from the corner of his mouth.

"You hungry? You had your supper yet?"

Kitch looked to Sammy, who he roomed with. "We gonna chow over there?" He motioned a thumb toward their other roommates sitting by a fire with a small kettle cooking something.

"Yeah, when it be ready, they call us," replied Sammy.

"You wanna share what I done made for me and Oscar?" She looked at Kitch then over to Sammy. "You too, Sammy."

"That'd be mighty fine," said Kitch.

With that, Mama went back to serve up the meal of soup and dry bread. Sitting out on our front porch, Mama asked Kitch how it was where he came from. According to what he said, it sounded like a decent place. Mama listened intently while Kitch did most of the talking, his tongue making a whistling sound as it slid through his missing front teeth.

Several nights continued like that, with Kitch coming around along with Sammy. A rapport developed among us, but I knew that his communication was guarded by the way he looked around to be sure no one else was listening and how he kept his voice hushed. After a couple of days, Albert came around. Mama was sure to say Albert was "a good and trusted friend."

As the friendship grew, Albert and Mama shared with Kitch what had happened to Pursey and reinforced that loose tongues had bad consequences. Most of the time, conversing was muffled and barely noticeable. At the end of Kitch's second month at the plantation, he mentioned a Negro lady who helped slaves escape. The whispered conversation with carefully chosen words stopped short when someone wandered near.

Kitch was a man who knew how to take things slowly. Another month slipped by with no mention of freedom or escaping. One evening, he appeared overly alert, looking around to be sure Prescott wasn't nearby with Buddy. He kept pausing between his sentences and interrupting himself; it sure seemed like there was more he wanted to say. But he took his time getting it out. Waiting for several seconds and raising his head to the relative quiet around us, he relaxed his shoulders, lowered his head and whispered to the ground. That's when he confided in Mama and Albert that he knew about "routes and places."

We all waited to hear what he meant by that.

He barely breathed a faint few syllables. He told us that the precious Bible of his that never left his side, well, it held a piece of paper in it. On it was a tiny map with the routes and places that helped runaway slaves.

After that night, it was hard to think of much other than those destinations where slaves were on their way to freedom. But the timing wasn't right. He told us so. And since he knew a lot more than we did about such things, we believed him.

So life continued, but with a new addition. Reading and writing lessons began. They continued and progressed until Sammy and I got all the way from A to Z and were able to pronounce some simple written words. Oh, the excitement I felt when Kitch taught me to write my name. Using a stick, I scrolled O-S-C-A-R in the dirt. The first time I ever saw my name in print made me swell with pride. Mama, too. Her smile was as bright as the noon-time sun.

Just around the fifth month that Kitch was with us, Mama whispered to me before we fell to sleep. "He a good man, that Kitch. So happy he learning you and, oh my, you catching on real good. Real good, Oscar." She gently wiped my fluffy black hair off my forehead.

The Day I Saw the Hummingbird

Hugging her as she embraced me for a goodnight kiss, with my arms still around her neck, I asked, "Mama, you think we can plan to be free?"

Her arms instantly straightened. I felt her tension, and I knew Mama feared my question. We had enough to fear knowing how the obedient slaves might be treated if the foreman decided they needed reminding who was boss. What would happen to a runaway slave who got caught? Mama always worried that the unknown was worse than what we already knew, no matter how bad reality was. That fear hung over her like a rain cloud. But I didn't entertain that same reaction. To me, the idea of freedom was exciting, an adventure. It was something new to dream about. I was way too young and naïve to believe that I was vulnerable like Pursey or the others who attempted to flee and were found, brought back, and punished. Or worse! Little did I know I would grow up fast. Too fast. And wise up soon. Too soon.

Mama ignored my question. "Time for bed now. Just be concentrating on writing that name of yours on the ground. And new words."

"Sure thing, Mama." I smiled into a sweet slumber.

Chapter Nine

The next morning, Mama was up early making breakfast. Waking up to her singing as she stirred the porridge made me smile. She was singing about a boy with brown eyes and sweet, smiling lips—making it up as she went along. She liked to do that, make up songs about all sorts of things. The sun. The stars. And me. Today she was going on about me, and how she loved how I looked. I never felt much about my face one way or another. I'd seen it in pieces of mirror that we had. My dark skin, straight, wide nose, and heart-shaped lips seemed plain enough to me. But to Mama, I was the most handsome thing alive. Her affections of heart blinded her to my countenance. It was no matter to me what I looked like. Nah, what struck me as important was what sat in my chest and how I felt about something. And that morning it felt good to hear Mama's chirping away like a happy bird.

Yes, the day started off on a happy note. Right down to the butterfly that came out of a stack of cut cane as I was bent over cutting. I couldn't keep my eyes off that beautiful creature, its bright orange wings with black stripes running through them like little veins and white tips capping them. It had the tiniest little head with two protruding antenna-like features. It flitted around making its work look so easy. I learned years later how caterpillars become butterflies. How that creepy-crawling, wormy-appearing, hairy thing turns into a beautiful, airborne, delicate beauty is something I still find hard to comprehend. Nature has never ceased to amaze me.

Out in the field, I couldn't help noticing things, like groups of ants. Hordes of them crawled by carrying twigs and tiny objects twice their body size. They reminded me of crop picking and the nonstop work. So much of what I'd witnessed in my young years in nature has stayed with me. And, before long, I'd be getting much more familiar with nature.

Slurping sounds took my attention off the bugs. Kitch was taking a drink. That man drank water by the buckets. Prescott didn't like us taking a lot of pee breaks, and it made me squirm to think of Kitch holding his pee in, sometimes for hours. I wondered if this was one of his natural-born talents or if he practiced at it. It sure seemed like a handy trick, and I decided to work on it in case I ever needed that particular skill if Kitch ever decided the time was right to escape.

We got back from the fields and had our supper before Sammy and I were out throwing rocks. Kitch came around and asked if we would like to learn to pronounce new words. We dropped the stones and went to sit by him. Kitch picked up a stick and wrote on the ground R-O-C-K. Confused, I shook my head unable to figure out how to say it when Kitch burst out chuckling. His low-pitched laugh made me giggle. We were both still laughing when he picked up a rock and asked, "What this?"

I looked at the rock and the letters on the ground. "Oh, Kitch! You fooled us." I hit Sammy's shoulder for impact. "Didn't he, Sammy?"

"Sure did. I ain't never seen that word, either."

That night I went to bed with Kitch's deep laugh echoing in my head. I smiled, and my sore muscles relaxed as I said goodnight to Mama.

"You doing good with Kitch, my little man," she cooed.

As I was approaching my eighth birthday, Mama stopped calling me her little boy. With my advancing age and new, although limited, reading and writing ability, I had earned the new distinction of being called a man. I didn't know it then, but soon she would be preparing me for the life of a fully-grown man.

What started out as a good day ended horribly. I shudder to recall the horrible event that would serve to accelerate what was brewing inside my mama's head about my future.

I was fast asleep but was awoken by a rustling at the door.

Thump. Thump. Thump. Crack!

The door to our cabin burst open, and there was Prescott with Smitty.

Mama shot up straight in her bed. She sternly commanded me, "Go to Sammy!"

Still confused and disoriented from having been abruptly awakened, I rubbed my eyes to regain my senses.

Prescott approached Mama, waving a whip while Smitty stood guarding the door.

"Oscar, go! Now!" I never heard her scream so loud before or since that night.

Without so much as putting on my shoes or grabbing my work clothes, I ran out. My heart was pounding in my throat. I could barely catch my breath by the time I got to Sammy's. He was fast asleep, along with Kitch and their roommates. Fear gave me chills as I tried to settle the knot in my gut that threatened to squeeze my last meal out of me. But the harder I tried to calm myself, the worse I felt.

"Sammy," I gurgled, saliva running down my chin.

"Huh," he grumbled and turned away to go back to sleep.

I swallowed hard to shove down the particles that I had heaved into my mouth. "Sammy!" I tried again. When he didn't respond, I raised my voice and shook him.

"What? Huh," Sammy lifted his head.

"Wake up! Something terrible—"

"Shh, pipe down!" A second man in the room whispered forcefully.

The others, including Kitch, remained snoring.

When Sammy was finally clear-headed, I muttered in his ear what had happened.

"Oh no!" he whispered.

"What we gonna do?" I cried, knowing what he would say.

"Nothing. Nothing we can do." He moved over and patted a small portion of his mattress. "Just try getting some sleep."

The Day I Saw the Hummingbird

Unfortunately, Sammy was right. He responded like I knew he would. Doing nothing probably kept us all alive. The ones who protested were tortured: they had water and meals withheld, they were whipped, beaten, chained, dragged by horses, branded; and some were raped. A few ended up dead—like Pursey.

I wanted to go back. I wanted to help my mama. I wanted to kill that bastard Prescott and his puppet Smitty. I wanted to take my nightshirt and tighten it around their necks and watch the life go out of them. I knew what they were doing to my mama. She never hurt a living thing, and I hated that this happened to her. I hated them. That hatred kept me awake until it was time to rise and go back to the fields.

Chapter Ten

It was clear from the sad expressions and the way everyone dodged conversations with me that word had gotten out. When around me, Mama sucked in her chest and tried to put on a good face. But all too often when her determination slipped, her tightened lips dissolved her forced smile. And when her forehead wrinkled and her eyebrows came together, then it was clear how much distress she was in. There were also the physical signs: cut marks, abrasions, and the bruises on her wrists that looked like they were made from tightly-knotted ropes. Those were the things she couldn't hide. And it broke my heart to see her stumbling to an erect position when she moved a load of sugarcane from the spot where she picked it to the pile of harvested crop. Every time I tried to help her, Sammy firmly grabbed hold of my shoulder to stop me. Later that night, he mentioned, "Makes it worse to draw attention. Just let her be. We all get through it somehow."

The Day I Saw the Hummingbird

He was right. There was also the fear that attention drawn onto Prescott's misdeed could fire him up. And that meant people got hurt. I never felt so helpless. I was fuming mad for days with nothing to work off my boiling steam but rock throwing at night with Sammy. With every throw, at every object, I imagined I was smashing a hard stone into Prescott's face, belly, chest, arms, legs, and groin. I imagined his bones cracking into pieces so he couldn't raise another arm to hurt anyone else ever again. It took me days to finally calm down. And while I was quieting my insides, Mama was planning something.

I was sure that the only spark left in her, the small light her eyes still held, was from what was going on in that head of hers. More and more, she spent time with just Albert and Kitch. Off they'd be in their own little corner chatting up a storm with one of them constantly looking around before resuming their wild pace of talk. When I tried to join, or Sammy tried to, we'd be shooed off. With a soft touch on my arm, Albert would say, "You boys go and play."

Their huddles went on for several nights before Sammy and I were allowed to join them. To my surprise, the first thing Mama brought up was that Kitch would continue teaching us to read and write. "You pay good attention for learning all you can," she said with a determination of attitude that lent no room for protest. There was something giving her strength that I didn't understand, but I felt pretty certain it wasn't just about my education.

* * *

I found out later that Mama was planning our escape. And part of that planning was to ensure things calmed down completely to avoid raising suspicion with Prescott or his gang. Everything needed to cool off and appear as if life was continuing as usual with no hints of unrest. Mama knew that Prescott was no genius and he'd rather be drunk than work hard. Giving the appearance that nothing was brewing, Prescott would relax his overly-active suspicious behavior and let his guard down. That was the first step of the plan.

As Mama gained strength of heart, determined to see me freed, she grew weaker in her body. Prescott did something to her that night that she never fully recovered from. I wondered if she had banged her head because she started to stumble and lost her train of thought more frequently than before he attacked her. With every changed and weakened gesture I noticed, my urge to kill Prescott resurfaced. When I'd see her normally steady hands shake at night, my anger made it hard for me to sleep. Out on the field each day and exhausted, I had to be sure to look away from Prescott, Smitty, or the rest of them for fear they'd see the hatred I held so tightly inside me. I thought my muscles would burst from the pressure of holding it all in. That's how my life and emotions went for days, moving into weeks.

My eight birthday came and Mama said it would not pass without celebration. She had some flour, crushed dried sugarcane, a couple of stolen chicken eggs, and a few other ingredients from which she made me a cake. It was big enough to share with Albert, Kitch, and Sammy. Sammy and I sat on the floor while Albert, Kitch, and Mama took up the mattresses. That cake made with love was the best I ever had.

While we ate and pretended a louder neutral social conversation, we carried on another murmured discussion. In those whisperings, Mama's plan was laid out. "No discussing this nowhere else," she said. "Never!"

Kitch nodded agreement while holding firm to his small Bible, the one with the escape route map hidden between a couple of the pages. Albert shook his head and whispered, "If only I be younger."

Sammy spoke a little too loudly when he replied with, "You strong. You can—"

Albert held his hand out at him to stop. He put a finger over his lips to indicate to keep it down and said, "Oh, this be a good cake, Cat." He then turned to Sammy and winked.

Sammy and I looked at each other, then back to the others, and nodded that we understood. "Yes," I smiled and said without hesitation, "I so happy you come for my birthday."

We all knew that two things were happening. We gathered for routine, "innocent" meetings about reading, writing, rock throwing, or things we learned out on the field about nature. At the same time, we engaged in hushed-toned survival training about paths, times to travel, things to be aware of, signs to watch out for, and how to fend for ourselves out in nature if things went astray during our journey to freedom.

We were clever. When we'd discuss how we'd seen bugs around the sugarcane in a normal voice, we'd whisper about insects and plants that we could eat if we ran out of food or didn't get to the shelter on the route in time to get a meal. The thought of eating crickets, beetles, grasshoppers, and even moths made me want to gag, but I had to get used to the idea in the shelter of my home. When Mama gave me a look and said, "Listen up, little man! You do what needs doing," I knew I'd learn to live with it. Or die trying.

As the meetings and discussions continued, I was filled with mixed feelings. Excitement mingled with sorrow. I'd be leaving my mama behind. In private talks at night before going to sleep when I tried to encourage her to come with, she told me that she couldn't. Her body wasn't strong enough. She would only hold Sammy and me back. When I whined, "I ain't going if you ain't going," she held my face in her hands, kissed my forehead and told me this was how it was to be. "And that be that, little man."

"Mama, I can help you."

"No," she replied.

"Then I gonna stay here with you."

"No." Her breath was strong in my ear when she continued. "I ain't gonna live to see something bad happen to my little man. You get yourself free. I want nothing else for my life. You go and find that freedom for both of us."

"Noooo, Mama," I moaned.

"Shh, now baby, you hear me," she sniffed. "You wanna make Mama happy? You do the plan. Sammy, he like your brother. You family."

"Mama," I cried the tears I knew she shared with me. "I love you, Mama. I love you!"

She grabbed hold of me and gave me a squeeze that took my breath away. "You my life. Long as you live, I live. You hear me?"

"Yes, Mama, I hear you."

"Well then, good. Time for sleep."

She stayed by my side until I fell asleep.

The Day I Saw the Hummingbird

Chapter Eleven

Months passed, and life continued as if everything was normal: the fieldwork, my rock throwing with Sammy, the gang chatting on the deck and privately in our cabin. So did Prescott's screaming and ranting at the workers, but for some reason, the physical abuse calmed down. His nighttime visits to our quarters stopped, too. Sammy was anxious for things to move along, but Mama and Kitch kept saying it wasn't time. Kitch told us about people called "conductors" who led or helped transport fugitive slaves from place to place. And what fascinated me was that some of these men entered a plantation pretending to be a freed slave looking for work, food, and shelter. Once a part of the working plantation, they'd help direct the path for the runaways. That was what Kitch had on that piece of paper he kept in his black book, a path to freedom. But since he wasn't a conductor and relied on things he'd been told, he was overly cautious in mapping out the final steps for our departure. Mama's obvious nervousness also held up our leaving. She always did like to tell me to slow down and appreciate the moment, but this was different. When her hands continued to shake harder and she couldn't wipe sweat from her forehead fast enough, I knew she was worried about me moving on with Sammy.

"How we know when the time be right?" asked Sammy. "I itchin' to get free once and for all."

"Hard to say exactly," Kitch responded. "Things stirring up since Mr. Lincoln took office. Big trouble brewing." I found out from Mama that Albert, along with her and Kitch, heard from Macy that the Colesons had talked about tensions rising up in the southern states.

As 1861 progressed and my eighth birthday was behind me, there was more than trouble on the horizon. There was downright danger with men leaving their plantations and homes to fight in the Confederate Army. The black man, considered property, was now the cause for a fighting nation. Everyone was involved in one way or another; either they were taking up arms, or they knew someone who was. The war came to the Coleson's plantation through close family of Mr. Coleson: a brother and nephew both enlisted to fight to preserve the southern way of life.

The map in Kitch's Bible was not just an escape route anymore; it was a battlefield. Although Sammy was ready, no one else agreed we should risk leaving. Our activities continued on as before while we pretended nothing was in the works. Pretending that everything was normal was hard on Sundays when Macy came around and updated us on things she had overheard. She told us there was one night she almost dropped a tray full of food when Mrs. Coleson said, "It's hard to fathom all the bloodshed. Chaining Negroes and dragging them like animals." Macy cleared her throat. "The missus said something else I couldn't make out then she done burst to tears and screamed at the master for telling her them awful things. Said she hated having them ideas floating around in that head of hers." Macy continued to tell us that they argued over the South having *blood on its hands.*

Unable to contain my curiosity, I barged in wanting to know more. "Blood?"

Mama nudged my leg, one of the many ways she let me know without using words that I should mind my mouth.

Macy looked at her papa. Albert nodded for his daughter to continue. "The master said all the hullabaloo over the niggers—"

"What's that mean, hullabaloo?" interrupted Sammy.

Albert shook his head like it wasn't important as Kitch looked around. Seeing that no one seemed to know, Albert shrugged. "Dunno, but it don't sound good."

"No, it don't sound good at all," continued Macy. "Mr. Coleson were upset 'cause of all the dying happening over what the North be doing."

"What the North be doing?" I asked.

Finally, Mama frustrated that Macy wasn't being allowed to finish more than two sentences, piped in. "Let Macy talk." She then gave my shoulder a gentle whack.

Macy's face grew downcast, and her shoulders slumped when she picked up with, "Mr. Coleson, he upset 'bout deaths of *his* kind. He say this and I remember 'cause it sound so bad! He say, 'niggers deserved to be hung up from trees, right along with their good ole northern friends. Slit their throats and feed them to the alligators. They ain't good for nothing else.' Lord Almighty, have mercy! Can you believe that? And the missus, she say 'South was just as much at fault, and it takes two to wage a war.' Master's face turn so red, I done feared for his wife." Macy continued on to say that Mr. Coleson shot up out of his chair and stormed out of the dining room, leaving his wife in a puddle of tears.

I was itching to ask a million questions but sat silently along with the rest. All eyes were on Macy who went on to say, "Stood there, right by the missus till she done pull herself together and left." Macy looked at her father, then the rest of us, and stated that she felt the missus was a nice lady with a good heart. "Mrs. Coleson's words, they carry kindness when she talk."

After a brief lull when Macy finished, Kitch spoke, "Wish more people be like that."

Macy nodded and mentioned that Mrs. Coleson would take time out to help her speak proper. On several occasions, she told Macy that she wished she could help her learn to read. The mister wouldn't allow it, so Mrs. Coleson did the next best thing: she helped Macy verbally when she could.

War talk persisted, and our plans were stalled. Sundays came and went and I turned nine years old. As Macy's visits continued, nastiness crept back into work with Prescott binging on the drink. And, sadly, he returned one night. This time it wasn't for Mama; it was for someone in the women's cabin. In the middle of the night, stinking drunk, he barged in with Buddy. The barking, growling, and screaming woke the whole quarter. The bloodbath didn't last too long before dead silence hung in the air like thick smoke. When it was all over, there was nothing left but carnage. The only survivor out of the five women was in shock. The next day she kept repeating, "That nasty man, he say this be for his kin murdered by some northern boy." This time Prescott was not so much as scolded by Mr. Coleson. Macy told us that Mr. Coleson said, "They deserved what they got. Too bad we can't kill them all and be rid of the scum, but we need them damn slaves to work to protect our land and make us money."

The heaviness in my chest made it hard to carry on. But the worst thing for me was seeing what it did to Mama. She trudged on like she was dragging her feet through thick mounds of mud. Seeing her bent waist, bowed head, and shaking hands (from the shock of it all), just broke my heart.

Four Sundays after that happened, we finally had a half-day off. We needed to leave behind the gloomy cloud cast upon us and move on—redirect our attention to what we could do to help ourselves. Our focus was back on the arrangements to free Sammy and me. That's when I found out that Kitch wasn't going with us. I had assumed that he would lead us since it was his plan we were using.

"How come?" I asked him in the privacy of our cabin while listening for intruders.

"Got me family where I come from. Don't wanna to go too far from where they is," he explained. Kitch, God bless his soul, helped us learn to read and write and selflessly shared a way to freedom with us. Mama was right about him from the start when she said he was a good man.

The Day I Saw the Hummingbird

Chapter Twelve

Macy's ears continued to buzz from the news she overheard by secretly listening in on conversations between the Colesons. Craning her neck around to be sure there were no sounds outside our cabin indicating an intruder, she was skittish in relaying information to the circle of five. Mama, Albert, Kitch, Sammy, and I listened intently to Macy's rapid-paced whispers. Stopping when she wasn't sure if she heard footsteps or any unusual noise outside, she shared the unhappy news about the geography Sammy and I would need to travel. Macy used a lot of new words she overhead in the main house: Civil War, Union Army, and others I can't remember because I got too nervous to listen.

While skirmishes were breaking out in the Mississippi Valley to retain control of the Mississippi River and war waged on, we looked at the choices for the best routes to take. All options intersected with sites where battles would most likely be fought. Although heavy fighting was yet way north of us, we learned that the Mississippi River, being the main artery of communication of the South and a vital link to Louisiana, would soon have the Union Army fighting to occupy its surrounding land. Thinking of the waterways and countryside crawling with soldiers did not make for easy breathing as we planned our escape. It gave me a sour stomach to think that we'd be heading straight into what would be a major battleground of the Civil War, the struggle for western waterways. And traveling near streams and tributaries could not be avoided. We needed the water to drink. And the fishing offered food when the limited supplies we could carry ran out.

Mama, ever brave (and with the support of Albert and Kitch), kept encouraging us to be strong. "You keep thinking of freedom. Breathe fresh air. Put faith in the Lord to see you through. And don't give up." Although her words were soft and sure, her hand wringing convinced me she was as scared as I was. But we were already living in fear every day. I could face my fear of the unknown and knew Sammy felt the same. He was itching to get going. My serious reservation was not for my life but for Mama's well-being. What would happen to her? Would I ever see her again? I knew the answer but didn't want to face it, and couldn't shake the dread from my thoughts or the sadness from my heart.

My introspection was interrupted when Mama's hand took hold of the map, gently lifting it from the Bible. The way she tenderly touched the book as if it held some magical powers brought me back to the moment at hand. Mama felt that the map was graced with the Lord's fine words, being that it was kept in the Bible. "This here map be holding the goodness of the Lord. Couldn't ask for a better piece of paper." Mama forced a slow smile and continued, "And that says it ain't no mistake it come to us right from that Bible."

Mama unfolded the brownish, stained map and we all looked at the lines and circles. Squiggles indicated hilly areas and waves were for rivers and lakes. On the top was N for north and at the bottom of the page was S for south. On the right side was E for east and to the left a W for west. I had no idea what north, south, east, west were until Kitch pointed east and said, "That's a big water area, called an ocean. Not something to drink. It real salty. Across that ocean be a whole other country." I don't know how that man came to be so smart. I assumed it was from the same son of his former plantation owner who taught him to read and write, where Kitch's family still was.

Also on the bottom of the map were little circles labeled berries that were safe to eat. Kitch mentioned that something called dewberries were tasty and abundant in Louisiana forest areas.

"How you know that?" Sammy scratched his head.

"Man by the name of Henry done come through to help us escape. Posed as a freed slave looking for work. Listened in a little when he be helping another fellow. He tell us all sorts a things in case something happen to him along the way so no one were gonna rely on him alone. Smart man, he was. Learn me 'bout these berries that be black or dark purple and look like a bunch of tiny round fruit. When you bite into them, out come a sweet juice."

"Like an orange?" asked Sammy.

We had oranges and apples but nothing like a small berry that I could remember.

"Suppose so, if the oranges be real small and lumped all together. And black." Kitch gave us a toothless grin. "Guess they ain't much like oranges 'cept they both juicy."

Mama smiled at Kitch's playfulness.

"I seen them berries," interjected Macy. "Mrs. Coleson has a cousin that grows them in spring and brings a basket along when she comes to visit."

"Never seen any here," I said.

"No, don't reckon they'd be shared with us. And that ain't a bad thing," Macy smiled. "They leave a stain on just about everything they touch. I couldn't get a napkin cleaned of that purple stain. Had to throw it out and was mighty scared I'd get in trouble."

Sammy laughed. "Bet you didn't tell nobody."

"No," Macy returned the giggle, "I sure didn't."

Albert put an arm around Macy's shoulder and pulled her closer to his side. "Let's let Kitch continue," he spoke warmheartedly into her ear.

Kitch then told us about so many things it made my head spin, like how he learned to make a spear to fish with. "Get a branch from a tree 'bout as thick as a thumb and—"

"Oh, Kitch," I interrupted, "how we ever gonna remember all you telling us?"

"Just do your best. Can't do more than that."

Mama nodded agreement. Albert smiled at Macy who was keenly listening.

We all looked down at that map, at tiny sketches that Kitch said were things to avoid: something with three leaves that can make your skin itch something awful and another plant. Pointing to that last plant, he said, "It got purple and white flowers that gonna make a body feel awful sick eating the flowers or chewing the leaves or stems."

"Sick like how?" asked Sammy.

"Henry, that there man I say before, tell it hurt your heart and make you vomit if you eat too much. Can even kill you."

"That be real sick," I gasped, fearing that I wouldn't remember a thing and eat one of those flowers.

Kitch noticed me shaking my head while holding my breath. "Best eat fish and critters. Don't eat plants unless you desperate. Then it be eat or die starving. And try sticking with berries or wild fruit you find."

I remembered from an earlier conversation that he told us about the places along the way where good people took in runaways to help them escape. These kind folks risked their lives sheltering and feeding my people. "But I thought there be places we stay and they feed us," I commented.

"Yes, if you lucky and everything goes all right. But if things go wrong..." Kitch looked at Mama, Albert, Macy, then Sammy and me. "If you get yourself lost, if the weather done up and change, or if there be danger and you stuck hid..." He didn't finish his thought.

Mama's neck muscles tensed into string-like coils. She grabbed my arm and firmly said, "You pay attention, you hear. Don't go marching into danger and don't be in no hurry to get yourself to where you won't never get to 'cause you in such a hurry."

"Yes, Mama," I looked at Sammy, who sucked in a slow breath through pursed lips.

"You listen to Kitch and mind him. He speaking for your life. This ain't no pleasure trip. This be your chance to stay alive. No knowing what gonna happen to us if that war come close to the planation. They might just burn us all alive."

I never heard my Mama talk like that, and it scared me. Her pupils were as big as a full moon, and her lips were as tight and small as a splinter. I knew she was afraid, too. Her fear gave her liberties and voice. Little did I know then that these words would stay with me forever, always reminding me to err on the side of caution. I'd repeat Mama's wise words inside my mind and give thanks to her for many years to come.

And the look on her face, the *don't you be disobeying me* demeanor, gave me both shivers and character. It was the strength of her love, the goodness of her selfless heart—the heart only a mother knows—that ultimately gave me courage. Mama gave me the wisdom to trust my gut, which I would have to rely on much more than I ever anticipated.

Chapter Thirteen

Hours slowly dragged on, moving into long days. My nerves were frayed, and I couldn't stop fidgeting, tapping my feet, and biting my nails. It got under Mama's skin. "Stop that fiddling," she hissed.

Sleep wasn't coming as easy as before. The talk of battles near where we'd be heading was too upsetting. To compound the tension that was squeezing my back muscles was the fact that all the planning wasn't going anywhere beyond hushed meetings. I was beginning to wonder if we were ever going to escape and blamed Macy for the reports she relayed to us about the fighting. Mama had changed her tune about my heading out and being strong. The hairs on Mama's neck were up when she told me, "You going nowhere till that fighting calms down." Her body shook when she continued, "No son of mine gonna rush into bloodshed."

I was getting tired of her wavering and demanding that, for now, no more plans be seriously considered. But

I didn't want to further upset her, so I surrendered and just answered, "Yes, Mama."

Sammy, eager to get a move on, wasn't helping when he urged me, "Forget all their worrying. Let's just get outta here." Out alone throwing rocks or sitting on a cut down tree stump chatting, we were plain frustrated with the standstill.

"Can't do that," I harshly whispered. "Ain't going against Mama."

Waving a hand in front of his face, he shooed a moth away. "What we waiting for?" He raised his voice.

"Shh!" I stood and kicked dirt to vent my annoyance. Just then we heard the sound of horse hooves approaching.

Sammy stood straight up and looked in the direction of the noise.

Clouds of dust surrounded two soldiers on horseback. One yelled, "Whoa!"

Acid rose to my throat when the other one galloped right up to Sammy and me, pointed a finger at Sammy and said, "You! Go and get two women slaves and bring them out here right away!"

Sammy's shaking legs stalled. "Yes, sir." He replied quick enough, but poor Sammy was frozen in fear. He just stood there.

"Did you hear me, nigger? Move or I'll do it. And if I do it, your neck will feel a rope around it! Now move!"

Sammy stumbled off. When he passed the cabin where Mama was making dinner, I breathed a sigh of relief until one soldier called to him. "Halt!" He pointed to my place. "Go in there."

Not my mama. Oh please, not my mama. Fearing the worse, my chest caved in on me. Sammy, taking his time, annoyed the man commanding him. "What the hell is taking him so long?"

Just then Mama came out wearing an apron over her dress. Sammy followed right behind her. She saw that I was banging a foot and kicking up dirt and gave me a look. Nodding her head to the side with lips drawn taut, she was trying to tell me to calm down. She then lowered her head and said nothing.

The man who ordered Sammy moved his horse closer. "Get another one."

With no hesitation this time, Sammy ran to the women's cabin and came out with a woman named Sally. He brought her back to where Mama and I were waiting with the two men on horses. The quieter one then spoke, "We need you to go to the main house. Men have been wounded and need tending to. Get on over there right now." With that, they turned and walked their horses next to Mama and Sally.

When they were out of earshot, Sammy whispered to me. "You see their uniforms?" He was referring to the tattered gray wool with a single row of half-torn-off buttons. They were covered in brown stains that looked like blood. "Looks like they just stepped out of battle." Sammy sucked in a slow breath and shook his head in disbelief. "Guess I was wrong 'bout what I said earlier."

"'Bout going?" I whispered back to him.

"Yeah, that near scared me to wet my pants. That look on that man's face, oh my—gave me a chill." He was referring to the one who gave the orders. The other one pretty much stayed back and was mostly quiet.

I knew what Sammy was referring to. I saw it as well. That soldier's chest was so puffed out I thought he'd pop the last two remaining buttons on his jacket. And those clenched teeth and eyes squinted like they were darting knives—that was the look of pure, unadulterated hatred. And Mama was being marched off to help more of them.

The Day I Saw the Hummingbird

I doubted that I'd get any sleep that night. But somehow I did. I woke up hours later at the usual time to go to work. Mama hadn't returned. Dressed and trying to force myself to eat a piece of stale bread, I felt too sick and frightened to get much into me.

Sammy and I walked in silence to the sugarcane field. For the rest of the day, we didn't say a word to each other. Prescott, in one of his states, intensified the dread I felt. Sauntering around with his rawhide whip in one hand and Buddy on the end of the leash in the other, he snapped that whip over our heads for no obvious reason other than his own amusement. And with the slightest reason to take out his hostility, he slapped it across a face, a back, an arm, or a leg of any slave near him. His mood was as sour as the acid I kept burping up from my nearly empty gut. I felt pity for the poor soul who dared to look up at him. That landed him a kick in the face with the back of Prescott's boot, breaking the man's nose. Prescott continued gulping down his liquor and screamed over to Smitty, provoking him to join in with the nastiness. Smitty, his peon, went along with it. So did Caulfield and R.J. That was a day of hell on earth for us. But what about Mama? I still hadn't heard a thing about what she was doing and when I'd see her again.

Just as the sun was dropping behind the edge of the earth, Prescott gave the order, "Ten more minutes." Then under his breath to Smitty, I overhead him say, "I should keep them all night. Let them starve for all I care. For all the trouble them niggers are causing our soldiers."

So that was it. He must have heard why Mama and Sally weren't in the field and about the wounded men in the main house that they were taking care of. Yes, he must have found out. And, in his usual obnoxious and pitiless fashion, took it out on all us innocents.

Chapter Fourteen

Early the next morning, Mama stumbled through the door. Having been in a light sleep, I instantly sat up and tried to focus my eyes through the dark room. She heard me stir and came to my bed. "Mama's home, my boy. We be fine," she sniffled. Her voice cracked with weariness as she softly reached a hand to my cheek and said, "I love you, my boy. My big handsome boy." She hadn't called me a boy in a long time, not since she felt I graduated up to being a *little man* capable of venturing out on my own.

"Oh, Mama," I threw my arms around her. "I'm so glad you here. What happened? Where them soldiers at?" I grabbed hold so tightly it made her cough. "Mama, what's going on?" A foul smell coming from her clothing made me want to gag. "I—"

"Shh now, calm yourself." She rubbed my shoulders with soothing, reassuring strokes that relaxed my tensed muscles. "Every little thing fine," she sniffled again and shook her head. A tear landed on my arm.

I swallowed the spit accumulating in my mouth. "You crying. Why you crying?"

"Shh, now. Mama's just tired."

"You been tired before but that don't make you cry. Please, Mama, tell me why. What happened over there?"

She clutched hold of my arms still around her waist and gave them a squeeze. A few seconds later she responded, "So much pain. Blood. Just dunno what to say. War ain't good for nobody. Them soldiers young, some looking none older than you." She mentioned overhearing a boy telling another wounded soldier he had just turned twelve and wasn't going to let his father go off to fight alone.

Being that I was nine and working the fields like an adult, it didn't surprise me one bit. Years later, I read something that mentioned in the South (in the years before the Civil War), half of all the slaves were younger than sixteen. We grew up early back then, if we grew up at all. To this day, it continues to pain my heart what was done to children. No wonder Mama didn't want to talk about those young soldiers, especially with Sammy and me making plans to leave. I sensed that her sobbing wasn't just about what she had seen but rather the heavy burden a mother carries over witnessing the daily oppressions, hardships, and horrors on her child and all the children caught up in the miseries of life. This was no life for any human being, let alone a child. I was so conflicted about what to do. I wanted to forget about leaving with Sammy and stay to watch over and comfort Mama. I wanted to tell her she had me for protection. I wanted to take away all her worries. But I knew what her response would be. The same it always was, *you grab onto your freedom and live a good life.* She would have given her life to set me free. That was my mama.

I was stuck between not wanting to make things worse for Mama and wanting to know what she experienced. Curiosity won. "What happened over there, Mama?"

She patted my back and let go of the grip she had on me. "Days of fighting are mighty hot. Soldiers in them heavy uniform sweat. Lost too much body fluid. They got sick." She told me that she had spent the better part of an entire day, along with Sally and Macy, helping to get water into the men. It had to be done slowly, or they'd vomit back up everything they just drank. The odor I smelled on Mama's clothing must've been from their vomit.

The Day I Saw the Hummingbird

Wondering about the soldiers' condition, I remembered being out in the field on especially warm days and sweating to the point of nausea and exhaustion. There were days when Buddy was tied to a tree under the shade with a bowl of water at his side while we were worked to the bone, losing our fluid and growing weak at the knees. And Prescott just watched. No one helped us to get water. We saw the glare on Prescott's face and didn't dare ask for even a drop.

I listened to Mama talk about the soldiers in their heavy wool uniforms, covered in perspiration and blood. Some with wounds she helped to bandage. She also mentioned that they'd been fighting not too many miles from the Coleson's plantation. Remembering discussions about routes Sammy and I would take, a shiver ran down my spine.

"You hear anything 'bout exactly where the fighting was?" I asked her.

Mama gave off a loud moaning sigh. She groaned deep in her throat, like she didn't want to continue the conversation. I knew that sound; it stirred up my interest even more.

"What'd you hear?" I knew she was holding back. What I didn't know was why.

The answer came the minute she started moving her lips. "Timing ain't right for you and Sammy to leave." She hesitated, sucked in a deep breath and continued, "Fighting be awful close."

"But, Mama," I let out a frustrated plea.

Reluctantly she pulled her shoulders back and softened. She explained about forts surrounding the French Quarter in New Orleans. I knew about the French Quarter from earlier conversations with Macy, about the comings and goings of the Coleson's visiting family and friends. Mama went on to say that she had overheard the talk about several forts protecting the big city that were swarming with soldiers. Several of the New Orleans residents, names we'd heard of from time to time: Beauregard, Braxton, and Taylor, were leading armies in the fields that would intersect with our intended routes. I suppose the silver lining of Mama's time tending to the dehydrated and wounded soldiers was that she learned a wealth of information that would prove to be extremely helpful for Sammy and me.

Unfortunately, what she learned also made her reconsider our plan to escape. She now thought the danger we would face outweighed the opportunity for our freedom. I hated causing her that worry. As if reading my

mind, she said, "Ain't nobody safe out there now. But…"
She patted my cheek the way she always did. Funny how
a simple thing like that can make a person feel comforted.
"Your freedom be coming. Just be patient, little man."

Chapter Fifteen

As the coolness started to disappear from the morning air, we knew it was time to get ready for work. I felt for Mama; she had had no sleep for two nights. When she lit a candle and began making breakfast, I could see her wrinkled face and bloodshot eyes. Everything about her was tired-looking. She appeared much older than her young thirty years. Oh, how I wished she could stay back in the cabin and rest. But no, she had no time for that. No time for anything other than grabbing a quick meal, feeding me, changing out of her putrid dress, and dragging her exhausted body to work.

It was an especially warm mid-May day. The hummingbirds had already arrived earlier that year. They usually welcomed in a new year, migrating to Louisiana around the end of January. Mama and I were working near the edge of the sugarcane crop close to some flowers when I saw a tiny bird dipping its long, slender bill into an orange bell-shaped flower. It was a rare treat when I spotted a hummingbird with its vibrant colors. Something about those birds made me feel more alive. I once tried to count the times one flapped its wings. I couldn't do it; it's near impossible to see the space between the movements. And oh, how that little beauty invigorated me. I thought the day had started off on a good foot, seeing that beautiful creature covered in the brightest turquoise blue I ever did see. The pretty little thing had splashes of orange on it, too—just like the color of the flower it fed on. I could surely fly off and spend the rest of my life living among such grand appeal. Mama was right when she would say, "It God's work in nature. You wanna find peace, my boy, God done filled the whole world with it. Just gotta look past all the folk who fuss and fume. God's creations, they is simple and fine." She'd smile and shake her head in amazement. "Proves to me," she'd sing, "there surely be a Lord creating all this." But what went wrong when that same Lord who created such magnificence also created men with bitter hatred in their hearts? I never got my answer to that question. And if ever there was a time I needed one, it would be the day I saw the hummingbird.

The hours moved slowly, and I worried about Mama who was sweating up a storm under the heat of the sun, which was large as a pumpkin burning bright in the sky. When she licked her cracked lips, I saw how dry her tongue looked. Not seeing any water in sight, I raised my head to get Smitty's attention to ask for a drink. Mama, catching notice of my antics, was thrown off balance. What Smitty noticed was Mama stumbling to regain stability and me instinctively extending a hand to help her.

Rushing toward us with his boots madly kicking up dirt and stomping on the sugarcane crop, he arrived with a scowl in his eyes. His face was pulled into a smug grin. "Get back to work!"

Smitty's loud voice caught Prescott's attention, and before I could so much as ask for a spoonful of water, Prescott slammed in on us with his whip. "What the blazes!" He looked at Smitty then cracked that whip on my back.

Ripples of sharp, stinging pain ran down my back. My lips twitched with burning anger that I held inside. I wanted to lash out and scream at them, but knew acting out would only make things worse for me, Mama and everyone else. When Prescott's attention shifted to Mama, I looked at her and clenched my fists.

Mama slightly tilted her hand with the palm facing me, indicating I should keep quiet. Her wide eyes and raised eyebrows said *don't react!* When she bowed her head, all hell broke loose.

With one hand, Prescott grabbed hold of the back of Mama's neck, jerking her upright to her feet. He hit her across the face with his free hand, sending her flying to the ground. "You stop working again, and it'll get worse." When she could hardly move, he kicked her hard in the ribs, taking the breath out of her and leaving her lying there covered in muck.

Buddy tried to lunge free from the shady tree he was tied to. Fiercely growling and pulling on his chain, it looked like he was going to break the tree in half.

Prescott then grabbed hold of Smitty's shoulder. "Don't let them get away with nothing." Just as he turned to leave, he paused, looked back at us and commanded, "No food or water for you two miserable lazy niggers."

Smitty nodded agreement. In a sickeningly sweet tone, he said to Prescott, "That'll teach them."

"It better." Prescott put a hand on his gun, gave a long smirking look to Mama and me, and then stomped off.

Smitty followed Prescott but stayed within sight of us. Standing in the shade, he took a swallow of liquor.

With my eyes fixed on Mama, I continued to cut sugarcane. She slowly moved from flat on her back, covered in soil, to her knees. Holding her hurt side, she tried to spit the dirt from her mouth, but there wasn't enough moisture to do much good. Using a part of the apron, she wiped away what she could. I'm sure it didn't do much good. Within a few minutes, she started to cough like she had something stuck in her throat. The pain in her side from getting kicked was probably making things even worse. Her breaths were short, fast, and shallow. When her cheek muscles started fluttering, I got scared she wasn't getting enough air.

All I could do was clench my jaw and keep to myself. She must have known I was boiling inside with anger. The *don't act up, my boy* looks she kept giving me worked. I just did my work and watched her when I saw that no one was watching me. Finally, when she got a long, slow breath in through her nose, my tensed-up back muscles relaxed a little. I continued on working and hoped that the day would end early. It didn't. Prescott kept us out in the field until way past sunset. When he decided to let us go, I grabbed hold of Mama's arm to help her back.

The first thing that came out of her parched mouth was, "You done good, my boy. I—" She coughed. Unable to finish her sentence through the coughing, I patted her back with my free hand. She grabbed hold of her ribs where that bastard physically assaulted her.

"You need to stop, Mama?"

In between choking fits, she barely said, "No, keep going. We both—" She tried to clear her throat, which sent her into more fits of hacking and wheezing.

"Don't try to talking anymore, Mama."

We made it back to our cabin and drank water. But that didn't stop Mama's coughing. Whether from the beating, the hot sun, the last two nights without sleep, or no water for way too long, she wasn't just reacting to dust in her mouth. She was ill. Throughout the night, she made harsh guttural sounds and hawked up phlegm. At first, it was white. When it turned from green to brown, I noticed her clothes were damp. She was burning up with fever. That night was spent with me trying to cool her down with a wet rag, helping her sip fluids, and keeping her sitting upright to make her breathing easier. She used to do that for me when I was sick with a cough, and I remembered it helped.

Finally, around what must have been just past midnight, she dozed off. So did I. The next morning, she seemed a little better but was in no shape to be out in the fields sweating and punishing her body. "Mama, stay back. I tell them you got the fever."

"No!"

"Mama, you not well. We gotta get word to Mr. Coleson for a doctor to see you."

"No." She coughed. This time, up came blood.

My stomach tightened into a knot. "That there." I pointed to the blood in her hand. "Mama, that bad."

"Just all that darn coughing. I good. We best be going."

"No!" I banged my foot down. "No, you need doctoring." I knew that Mr. Coleson usually liked us to try home remedies before getting a doctor to come out to see us, but I didn't want time to waste before Mama got help. And since there was no infirmary on his plantation like with some of the other ones I'd heard about, I wanted Mama to be seen by a doctor.

"You listen here. The master don't like doing that, and you know it. Cost him time and money," she weakly scolded. "I fine. And that be that."

"Mama, please," I moaned.

When she saw me tearing up, she eased her tone. "You do that and Lord knows what that nasty man gonna do next time he see us. Too much trouble these days with folks warring and all." She raised an arm to me. "Now help your Mama up."

"At least take the day off and rest, drink..." I protested one last time.

She wasn't having it. When Mama dug her feet in, there was no talking sense to her. She could be as stubborn as deeply rooted sugarcane stuck in the ground. But she had a point about Prescott. And the risky times with the war going on. Since she was doing a little better than in the middle of the night, I gave in. Plus, I didn't want to aggravate her further, but I was worried. Especially after seeing the blood.

A flicker of something unclear flashed across her face. I wondered what it was. When she rotated her head to loosen her neck muscles, lifted her shoulders, and puffed out her chest, I knew my answer. It was courage— the strict parent to fear. But all the courage in the world would not remove the horrible seeds that were planted in Mama's body the day I saw the hummingbird.

The Day I Saw the Hummingbird

Chapter Sixteen

That day was a disaster. I knew the minute we set foot out the door. My arms begin to itch. Mama used to tell me I'd break out in a rash on my arms when I was a baby. She said she thought it was from nerves. The first time it happened was after my papa died.

Storm clouds of doom were gathering. I wish I had listened to my gut screaming at me to keep Mama put. But my mama was so strong-willed it was near impossible to change her mind when she had it set on something. The more I thought of Prescott, the more I rubbed and scratched my itching arms until they broke out in bumps. *Why can't he leave us alone to get on with our work? Why is his soul so filled with poison?* My mind found unanswerable questions as Mama and I made our way among Sammy, Kitch, and Albert to the sugarcane field that seemed a million miles away.

Thank God for Kitch who finally said, "Cat, you looking gray in your skin. How you feeling?"

Pigheaded Mama just gave him a look and kept on moving until her knees buckled. Kitch and Sammy caught her by the elbows to hold her up. "We ain't taking you out there." Kitch nodded his chin toward the sugarcane. Then he looked to Albert, "Go on and tell Prescott that we taking Cat back to her room. She too ill to work."

Sammy raised a questioning eyebrow to Mama and asked, "You want me to go tell Mr. Coleson we need a doctor?"

A harsh whispered "No!" was all she was able to mutter before her breathing became labored and she coughed up some thick brown stuff that looked like dried mud.

My Adam's apple bobbed up and down in a hard swallow. The frantic beating of my heart pulsed blood to my legs. *Run! Run! Go get Mr. Coleson to get the doctor* was my only thought. No more abiding to Mama's weak commandments. My burning arms felt like they'd fall off if I didn't get Mama help fast. Tears rolled off my cheeks as I bolted toward the main house, leaving the others to get Mama back to our cabin.

I made it to the large front door, which I later found out was not where slaves were supposed to go. I had no idea about the servants' entrance, nor did I care at that moment. Anger boiling up in me, I chewed on my lower lip as I madly pounded on the door. Howell, the butler, answered. I didn't know this man. Some of the slaves that worked the main house lived in quarters away from ours, and we never saw them. He took one look at me, sweat and tears dripping down my face, and with a hint of irritation said, "Servants don't—"

"My mama be sick!"

He pointed his chin up in the air and motioned to the right side of the residence. "If you'll just go around."

The belittling look he gave me went right off my back. "She really sick. Coughing up blood!" I screamed so loudly that Mrs. Coleson appeared at the door behind Howell. She was a stunning sight in a beautiful, full, emerald-green satin dress with puffed sleeves, a lace bodice, and shoes so shiny I could see a reflection in them. Hours later when I calmed down, I recalled how she looked. I'd never seen a real lady dressed up in all her finery. A fine, good-looking woman she was. But also, a kind woman, like my mama. In the years since then, I grew to understand that beauty isn't defined by the clothes we wear but by our inner goodness that radiates out and shines like a light that can brighten the darkest moments. Just the way she carried herself made me feel calmer. I sensed I could trust her to help my mama. Not like that awful Prescott.

The butler tried to intervene. "I was just trying to tell this here young man to go around—"

"Never mind that, Howell." Mrs. Coleson then gave me her attention. Without enquiring as to my name, she instantly asked, "What seems to be the trouble?"

Managing a calm tone and manner that shielded what I was really feeling, I pleaded. "My mama be ill, ma'am." I straightened my shoulders. "Very ill. Ma'am. She need a doctor, Mrs. Coleson. Please."

She was instantly distracted by a noise behind her. It was Macy. Eavesdropping. She failed to conceal herself adequately, so Mrs. Coleson called her over. "Do you know this young man?" She asked in a concerned tone, as if needing verification there may be a serious issue at hand.

Lowering her chin, Macy glanced down at her shoes. (I wondered if she felt guilty she was caught eavesdropping.) "Yes, missus, his Mama were here the other night with Sally. They was helping the soldiers."

"The nice older woman?"

She must have been referring to Mama since Sally was years younger.

Macy raised her head, her eyes wide and sad. "His Mama, she a good woman." I detected a trace of fear in her voice. She continued. "She work very hard, like Oscar—her boy here."

Mrs. Coleson looked at Macy's sorrowful expression and servile stance. The missus then turned to me. With gentle softness, she said, "My husband is away for a couple of more hours. I'll have him fetch Doctor Johnson when he returns."

I stammered a thank you. As I turned to leave, the missus caught my attention. "Oscar."

I pivoted around. "Yes, ma'am."

"You go and be with your mama. I'll get word to Mr. Prescott."

I tipped my hat to her. "Thank you, ma'am. Thank you." I clenched my jaw to hold back the tears that wanted to flood out of me and ran as fast as my legs would carry me back to Mama. When I got to our place, she was fast asleep, snoring a loud rattling noise that gave me a stomachache. It didn't sound right.

Kitch had stayed with her, refusing to leave, and I knew he'd suffer for that. He told me she fell on the bed the minute they arrived back. She had a cool rag on her forehead. One touch of her hand told me the fever had returned, worse than before.

"Kitch, the doctor's gonna come. You go on to work. I'll stay with Mama."

He nodded. Put a hand on my shoulder, shook his head, and said, "She a good woman, your mama. She strong and she gonna get through this." His face was clouded in worry.

The longest hours of my life passed while waiting for that doctor. Painfully, minutes ticked by, and I waited to hear horse hooves. Finally, at what must have been three hours later, Doctor Johnson arrived looking like he hadn't slept in days. It dawned on me that he must have been tending to soldiers. He looked overworked and overwhelmed but he, like Mrs. Coleson, seemed a kind person, sympathetic and soft-spoken. And just the fact that he stopped by to see a slave with all the goings-on told me that Mrs. Coleson must have had a hand in it. I will never forget her compassion in helping Mama.

Doctor Johnson wore a dark suit and carried a case with his supplies in it. He went to Mama and lifted her limp hand. I was surprised she slept through it. And scared. My mixed emotions were tugging at me from every angle: I was glad she was getting rest, but my mama was a light sleeper. Here was a stranger touching her body and she didn't respond. He felt for pulses and commented, "Her heart is fine. Not weak, but beating a little too fast." He gazed into my eyes when he spoke then put his attention back to Mama. "It's fast because she is burning up with fever."

Mama let out a rattling, gurgling cough and up came that thick brown phlegm. When she moaned without opening her eyes, I whispered close to her ear, "Doctor's here, Mama. He's gonna take care of you."

Doctor Johnson observed the mucus and smacked his lips like he didn't like the looks of it. He then pulled a wooden cylinder out of his bag and placed it over Mama's chest. He put an ear to one end and listened to her breathing. From where I stood, I could hear the wheezes and gurgling. It didn't sound good. Not good at all. "Her lungs are full of fluid," he said.

"What does that mean?" I asked.

He said the word *pneumonia* and went on to explain that Mama's lungs were filled with pus. And unless we could get the pus out, there'd be no room for air to get in.

"Like drowning?"

"Yes, son. But in her own fluids."

The Day I Saw the Hummingbird

A wave of dizziness filled my head. A hot flush moved through my limbs. The itching on my arms grew so intense I wanted to rip them out of their sockets. And I wanted to scream, *help her! Help my mama!* But I knew from the way he cleaned off his instrument, slowly put it away, and then sat beside her quietly that there wasn't anything he could do. Nothing any of us could do.

Mama would tell us to pray.

Even though I feared the answer, I had to ask, "She gonna get better?"

He gently responded, "Only God knows." He patted me on the back, straightened his coat and picked up his case. As he plodded out the door, he gave me a pitiful goodbye look.

Chapter Seventeen

Sitting beside Mama, I felt faint from the heat rising in the room. It was another warm early afternoon in May. Since I wasn't used to being in our enclosed cabin during the day, I didn't realize how stifling it got. The warmth coming off Mama's body added to the temperature. When the cool wet rag on Mama's forehead turned lukewarm, I took it off, soaked it in cooler water, and had a drink. I sipped the liquid, letting it run down through the lump in my throat—the one that formed and grew with each labored breath Mama took. As I watched Mama struggle to breathe, my chest felt tight. I wondered if this was how hers felt. But my lungs weren't full with sickness. They were cramped from the strain of holding back tears that hadn't reached daylight. If somehow she was aware of my presence, I didn't want to cry and upset her. She was never happy seeing me upset. For different reasons, it was hard for both of us to breathe.

When my belly gurgled and hunger distracted my attention, I put the cooled rag back on Mama's forehead and grabbed a handful of chushie. That sweet fried cornmeal cake was left over from the last meal she made before tending to the soldiers. I picked off the tiny fuzzy green parts and smelled it. It hadn't started to smell bad, so I knew it was still good to eat. There were times when we had to eat putrid-smelling food. Sure enough, a few hours later, our innards would be in an uproar. It was awful having the runs while working the field.

For the better part of the day, Mama continued to gurgle and cough. Once or twice she'd moan or writhe into spasms like she was trying to clear her way to taking a breath. Holding her up to help, my arm felt the intensity of the fever raging through her body. "I'm here, Mama, I'm here," I whispered in her ear. "Your little man, Oscar, he here." I kissed her burning cheek. "You get well Mama. You hear me?" *Please, Mama, get well.*

Finally, in what felt like days, the room started to cool. The setting sun told me that the workers would soon be coming back. Before long, I heard a set of footsteps on our porch. The door creaked open and in popped Kitch, followed by Albert and Sammy. Kitch approached concentrating on Mama and asked, "How she doing?"

Albert shook his head slowly. Sammy kept quiet as well. They came closer to the bed wearing frowns they didn't try to hide. Kitch put a firm and reassuring hand on my back and gave it a rub. With my eyes back on Mama and the three of them behind me, I said, "I just dunno." Feeling their kindness and attention flowing down on me as I sat beside her made the dam in my chest want to burst. I sniffed in a quick breath to shove down what was threatening to gush forth.

Kitch attempted to comfort me. "She a strong woman. She gonna come through this."

Albert and Sammy remained silent. I could hear them breathing a much slower rhythm than Mama's rapid, shallow pants.

After a few minutes, Albert spoke. "You need anything? Something to eat?" The nurturing father in Albert sounded through those words, like the tone my mama used when taking good care of me. It was all I could do to just simply shake my head *no*.

Feeling choked up, I cleared my throat, stood, and turned around. "Why don't ya'll go and grab yourself something to eat? I'm fine here with Mama."

Then Sammy piped in. "How 'bout you take a break and lemme sit with her?" Mama was like a mother to

Sammy. He loved her and loved hanging around with us. It was no surprise she picked him when she had my escape to freedom in mind. It'd be like having family, a brother, out in the wilderness taking care of and helping me. I loved Sammy for offering and knew it would make him feel good to help her. I gently patted his strong upper arm muscle and moved aside for him to sit beside her.

"Come on out," Albert took hold of my elbow. Outside with him and Kitch, I felt lonely. My heart was on that bed in that small room watching every breath Mama took, praying there would be another. And another. I prayed that with each new breath she'd grow stronger and open her eyes to smile at me. I longed to look into her big, brown, beautiful, expressive eyes that showed me so much love and concern. She always wanted what was best for me. The best thing in the world for me would have been for her just to get better.

Out on the porch, Albert looked to the bright, nearly-full moon lighting the night. It was good of him to change the conversation, shifting to harmless talk to give me a needed rest from all the nervousness pulsing through my weary body. "Look at that there big round light up yonder. Ever wonder how far away it be? Or what be going on up there? Maybe right now there be people looking down and wondering who we is," he said.

What I noticed next was not the moon, sky, stars, or any other heavenly body, but Kitch sniffling. Snorting through his nose, his mouth wide open to catch a breath, he was whistling through the space between his missing teeth. It reminded me of that first day we met him and how Mama scolded me to wash my teeth so they wouldn't yellow and fall out like his did. At that moment, the color of my teeth didn't matter. I was just glad to have Kitch and Albert by my side. They reminded me of the good things, times with Mama filled with laughter, song, and happiness. Albert and Kitch were a big part of those times. Especially on the day Kitch offered the promise of hope when he shared his map, when he gave Sammy and me the way to freedom. And as if he read my mind, he reached to the back of his dungarees and took his Bible out of a large pocket.

"Here," he handed it to me. "I want you to have it."

Pulling my hand back, "Kitch, I can't take your Bible."

"Got my use out of it. Now it gotta find a new place to be of value."

The Day I Saw the Hummingbird

With that, the dike burst and out came the flood of grief I was holding in. On and on, it came pouring out of me. With two of my best friends beside me, the other one in with Mama, I sobbed my heart out. I took the Bible and held it to my chest as if to catch the deluge coming out of me. Or maybe to help cover the hole in my heart that had been ripped open ever since the day I saw the hummingbird.

I didn't know it then, but the Good Book wasn't what Kitch really wanted me to have. He wanted to make sure I had that piece of paper inside it. That was the gift he gave to me on that fateful day.

Chapter Eighteen

A bloodcurdling scream from Sammy hit me like a sharp knife jabbed right in the middle of my forehead. I jolted upright, not sure if Mama was better or worse. Although it didn't sound good, I wasn't going to jump to that conclusion. I didn't want to assume the worst. I couldn't.

The minute I saw Mama's pale gray complexion, I had my answer. In the short time I was outside with Kitch and Albert, it looked like something had drained the life out of her naturally beautiful coloring. Still unconscious, she was gasping for air. Then, as if seeing a ghost, she gurgled, "Mack." My papa. Mama's lips puffed and out came a barely perceptible, "I hear you, Mack." Her voice trailed off. Then, as if time itself was suspended in very slow motion, she snored in a loud rattle. When her vacant eyes opened, staring at nothing, I felt cold. I had seen that empty look before—on Pursey hanging from a tree. Moist froth ran down her chin before her head went limp. So did my soul.

The Day I Saw the Hummingbird

The others wanted to stay but I told them, "No, I wanna be alone with my mama." Not a word was spoken before the door gently closed behind them. I sat by her until the last of the heat in her body went cold and her skin looked rubbery. Lifeless.

My mama's death was not real to me. *This can't be. She gonna wake up.*

I waited.

I hoped.

Maybe somewhere in the heavens there was a miracle to be had. But Mama didn't ever talk about miracles even though she was always going on about God and the Lord. Nah, she'd tell me to buck up and keep going. Or I had to be a big man now because I was ready. She was a no-nonsense kind of woman who never had time nor patience for talk of miracles. I wanted my Mama back in the worst way, but I wanted to make her proud more than anything else. I had to make room in my broken heart for the courage to make my Mama proud.

But I felt something else occupying my grieving heart: Prescott. That bastard caused all this to happen. On the day when I saw the hummingbird, when I thought all would be right in the world, he ripped my heart out. The only thing that made me feel any better was my hatred for that despicable excuse for a human being. As much as my mama taught me about love and the kindness that a good heart can bestow upon another, Prescott had taught me how to hate with a burning passion that made me want to kill him. The empty ache in my soul that he caused was now filled a poisonous bitterness that consumed me.

Breathe, I told myself. I made myself take in a few slow breaths through my nose. *Calm down.*

Just as I rose to get Sammy to help me bury Mama, I heard her voice. It was animated and alive. Was my mind playing tricks? But the words weren't just my imagination. They were a guiding force. *Don't you ruin your life, your chance at freedom.*

I reached into the air to find the space I thought her words were coming from. "Mama," I spoke to the room, empty of all but her dead body. I stomped on the floor to be sure I wasn't caught in a horrible nightmare. "Mama, I hear you."

Then, as if by divine intervention, my fingers moved to the gift that Kitch gave me. Again, I heard Mama's voice of reason say, *Your life be a gift. You keep on living and get yourself north. Go with Sammy.*

I rubbed my hand over that Bible like Mama did the day we learned about the map it held. *The gift of the Lord* she called it, a validation of the Lord's goodness. Where was that God now?

Conflicting emotions battled in my head as I went to get Sammy to help me dig a grave. The digging tired me out. And it calmed me down. When we were done, and my mama rested next to my papa—in the earth she so loved to say was God's soil—Sammy and I sat down. He tossed a rock and a fleeting sweet memory of better times moved before me.

Sammy wasted no time when he said, "Kitch tell me 'bout the gift he give you."

"Not now, Sammy." And then I heard a rattling sound, like twigs breaking or a dog's paws moving near. I jolted up to my feet, startling Sammy. "You hear that?"

"No."

Holding my breath and in absolute stillness like a prey animal, I waited.

Nothing.

I sat back down after a few minutes. "Musta been my imagination." I was sure it was Buddy…and Prescott. But the thought of that dog at the end of the leash held by the man I despised snapped me out of my resistance to making plans with Sammy so soon after we had just buried Mama. *You let Prescott poison get into your system and he win,* I recalled Mama's advice. *You hold on to them bad feelings and you only hurting you. It ain't hurting Prescott, Oscar,* she would say. *He like that. Don't give him no joy of thinking he control your soul like that.* My mama's womb had given me life, but it was her wisdom implanted in my brain that kept me alive.

An evening breeze filled the air. The wind picked up, blowing clouds across the moon. Feeling my mama's love filling me, I patted the dirt covering her grave. "That gift?"

Sammy nodded.

"We gonna share it, Sammy." In case anyone was in earshot, I spoke in secret communication to conceal the actual meaning.

"You sure?" But before even letting me answer he responded, "Good to hear, Oscar. Mighty good."

"Yep, we need to add it to them daily lessons. Starting tomorrow." A lot of the folk where we lived knew Kitch was teaching us reading and writing. For the benefit of safety, we always referred to the lessons when we wanted to talk about the map and our plans to flee, which would be put into motion very soon.

Chapter Nineteen

Aching over the loss of Mama, I felt conflicting and shifting emotions. A huge part of me felt empty and brokenhearted; another part felt disgust and anger. I was also determined to get on with the plans for freedom started several months ago.

Get up. Dress. Keep with the routine. Focus on one action at a time: one simple movement then the next. But keep busy, because if I didn't, I was sure to go mad and seek revenge. Sitting by her freshly dug gravesite with Sammy and recalling my mama's words, I was convinced that an *eye for an eye* approach with Prescott wouldn't do any good. The best action was to stick it to that cruel excuse for a human being by gaining our freedom. Just the thought of him fuming over escaped slaves gave me a bit of relief. I had to do what I could to keep my mind from sinking into a permanently grim pit of vengeance and destruction. If not for myself, then for everything my mama stood for and wanted for me.

I forced myself to eat the last of the chushie she had made. More green fuzz had grown on it and it had started to smell foul. I didn't care. It was simply fuel to keep me going until Sammy and I left. When that dried cornmeal cake stuck to the roof of my mouth, I pressed my tongue against the thick mass to remove it. The harder I pressed, the firmer it became. I gulped a swig of water and swished it around, but that darn food wouldn't budge. It was stuck to me like the anger I felt for Prescott. The more I tried to free that piece of crust, the more it clung to the roof of my mouth and the madder I became. Frustrated, and with tears dripping down my cheeks, I picked up the first object I could reach and threw it against the wall. When I came to my senses, I saw it was one of Mama's shoes. "No!" I screamed. Her unworn clothes came into focus. I saw the indentation on her mattress and pillow. It was evidence of her life. Evidence of her. A flood of grief came forth.

Use a piece of material to clean your teeth, Mama's words echoed in my head. *Don't let them yellow.* I ripped a piece of cloth that was on my bed and worked it around the place the mush had stuck. It freed and so did the last of my held-back crying. Although my body felt lighter from the release, my heart still felt like it was in a vise that had squeezed the life out of it.

When Sammy knocked to come get me to walk to the field, I was still barefoot. I grabbed my shoes and followed him, neither of us saying a word. My bare feet were a slight hindrance, and I was unable to keep pace. I stopped to put on my footwear. Sammy slowed and turned around. "Go on," I motioned to him with my hand.

"Just hurry and get them things on." He wouldn't budge. There was something about that small gesture of waiting for me that felt huge to my aching soul. I loved that man. So did my mama.

Sammy saw me smile. The worry lines around his mouth disappeared. His lips softened and turned slightly upward, but not enough to betray the pain and emotions we were both feeling. The delicateness in his facial expression reminded me of Mama. The way she looked at me with her soft, teary, brown eyes, the whites filled with bloodshot and weariness. The way she would comfort me even when she needed comfort. The way she put me and others first, above her exhaustion and needs. The world was a far better place with her in it.

* * *

Immersed in the crop, I was crouched on my knees cutting cane. My sweaty hand lost grip on the blade before it fell to the ground. I reached down to grab it and continued sawing at the base of the root when Prescott tromped over spewing a spray of dirt into my face. Blinking to clear my eyes, I continued cutting. I tried to keep my focus on my work, but there was no way to avoid him. He was breathing heavy, tapping his thick-soled boot in the loose ground right next to where I was working, and guzzling what must have been liquor. Feeling hostility rise up in me with every tap of his boot in the dust, I held my breath just hoping he'd move on. But no, he was there to stick it to me.

"Hey, Clawson. Think you can keep your sweaty black paws on that there knife and do your damn job?" He sneered. "You lucky little nigger. But trust my word, you give me one excuse to kick your butt, and you're a dead nigger."

I had no idea what he was referring to. *Lucky?* I almost lost control. It was all I could do to refrain from taking that knife and plunging it into his cold, empty heart. Prescott, still behind my back, couldn't see what my hands were doing. I grabbed onto that blade and squeezed the handle so tightly that my knuckles turned lighter. Venom flowed through my limbs as an urge to settle my score with him battled with the ounce of sanity still present in my head. *Don't be doing nothing foolish.* Mama's words came to me, balancing the silent struggle raging between my ears. As Prescott trod off, I loosened my hold on the cutter, continued working, and willed myself to get my mind off that despicable man.

Several days later on Sunday when Macy came to visit, I found out what Prescott meant by my luck. It seems that Mrs. Coleson had given strict orders to be passed along to the field staff that I was to be left alone. Macy told me, "Don't you be worrying about anyone messing with you or anyone who helped your mama." Her eyes teared up when she continued. "When the missus found out your mama passed, she was mighty upset."

Hearing that Mrs. Coleson reacted that way surprised me. I never imagined or expected it would have had that kind of impact, that Mama meant something special to a fancy white woman. Just knowing about that would carry me through the next few days. I needed to lie low while the skirmishes were moving north. Macy had kept us informed about the fighting. A few days back, she had overheard that the immediate area surrounding New Orleans' forests and trails had fewer soldiers. Battles had shifted north, which meant we could leave anytime and be a couple of days behind them. Waiting two more days would give us even more time and a better chance of safe passage.

The days we stalled and stuck around the Coleson plantation were awful. Whereas Prescott left me alone, he became an even less predictable madman with the others. Not that he was all that predictable to begin with, but at least we knew what things set him off: talking back, not working to his liking, or not meeting quotas for example. His drinking intensified, and he used any excuse to brutalize workers with whippings, withholding food and water, forcing himself on women, and using Buddy to scare the daylights out of children just for fun. With every injustice I witnessed or heard of, I dug my nails into the palms of my hands, drawing blood. I was now more determined than ever to get the hell out. I regretted that so many would be left behind to suffer, but saving everyone was something I didn't know how to do. I wasn't even sure Sammy and I would make it.

Kitch, Albert, and Sammy kept me company at night. Kitch continued teaching new words and even explained to Sammy and me that there was another good book. It was called a dictionary. He said, "When ya'll are free, you get yourself a hold of one and learn lots of new words." I've never forgotten that advice. It was the beginning of my keen interest in studying the importance and power of words. I came to understand that it wasn't just horrendous abuses to a person's body that cause pain. The things we say can be terribly hurtful, too. I've seen the result of abusive words in scars like bent heads, tortured eyes, and slouched shoulders. To this day, I do my best to use words to speak my mind with clarity and consideration. I try to present myself with pride and self-respect and extend that respect to others. That is pretty much all I can offer the world other than a smile and acting kindly.

During the last couple of nights before we left, I remained alone in our cabin. I wondered if Mrs. Coleson allowed me to stay put and not move into the men's cabin. For whatever reason, whether intentional or oversight, I was glad to have that time to myself. I used to envision myself talking to Mama. In the dark, I'd pretend she was with me like before. And the power of my mind did bring her to life for brief periods. It helped me to cope. It made me feel better. In my imagination, I'd converse with her and plan what I needed to pack to ready myself for the trip.

"What food you gonna take, my little man?"

"Oh, things I still have here. Cornmeal, mandingo (similar to spinach), hominy corn, rice, black-eyed peas, and yams."

"Lordy, sounds good!"

"And Macy is fixin' to bring some food from the Coleson's kitchen."

"Bless her sweet soul."

"Yes, Mama. I'm lucky with friends."

"You sure is." Mama's voice would grow weaker and trail off with a whisper. "Now, go on. Just keep your head and find your freedom."

When I would finally return to reality, I felt better. The line between Mama's wisdom and my wisdom was becoming blurred. I *was* sure lucky with friends. Especially Kitch. He wrote new words in the dirt to fake a lesson, but he continued to teach us about being out in nature and fending for ourselves. He reviewed what he had taught us about making weapons to catch critters and fish. He showed us again how to make a spear, how to make twine into a rope, how to make a lasso, and how to start a fire.

"Remember," he said with a wink, "there's no shame in cuddling together to keep warm." He paused a couple of minutes and appearing uncertain hesitated with squinted eyes, then continued. "Best to carry a knife. It be a mighty good friend in all kinds a fixes." He pulled his out and stroked its handle as if it were a beloved's cheek. *I gotta remember to bring a knife.*

In those earlier years, when we were planning on the right time to leave, I grew up fast. Mama used to say I had inner wisdom and people knew they could trust me. I think that's why she and Kitch spoke things to me at an early age—like the escape plan. They never treated me like I was just a child, incapable of understanding adult things.

Even with all the faith Mama and Kitch seemed to have in me, I was scared. I might forget what Kitch told me. Maybe I wasn't ready to be out on my own, even with Sammy? I was worried we wouldn't find any of the houses marked on the map—with squares and *X* marks— the safe places along the Underground Railroad. But what options did I have? Stay and be tortured or leave and brave it.

No. I had to leave. The choice was made for me the day mama died.

The Day I Saw the Hummingbird

Chapter Twenty

Sammy and I decided to wait a week and leave the following Sunday when we had a half-day off. That would avoid Prescott maybe making the slaves—including Sammy and me—work late the day we planned on leaving. We wanted to be as sure as we could that everyone would be in bed asleep and not staggering in from a late day in the field. We were gambling that it would be a *real* partial workday.

The night before we were to leave, I made a sack out of a bedsheet and packed some clothes: an extra pair of coveralls, a thick cotton slipover shirt, two pairs of socks, two pairs of underpants, an undershirt and sweater (in case it got cold). I planned on wearing my work shirt, pants, hat, socks, and shoes. I also made another pouch out of a pillowcase for carrying food and a knife. I put in it what I already had, and I also included a small leather satchel Kitch gave me for storing water. He brought it with him from the former plantation. When he told me,

"You take this here sac for water," his huge, toothless smile grabbed hold of my heart. I hugged him. He had given me his two worldly possessions: the Bible and his water container. After inserting the Bible among my clothing, there was a little room left in the food bag for anything Macy might bring from the big house kitchen.

I finished packing and looked around the only place I'd known as my home for almost ten years. It was hard to imagine never returning. As I had every night since Mama's death, I went to visit her grave. This time it was to say goodbye to her physical location. I would never leave behind my love for her, the bond I felt, and our connection that gave me strength. She used to say that about the Lord—that He was her strength. Maybe my love for Mama was setting me on a path to finding God? Right then, it was hard to know much of anything for sure other than my deep and undying feelings for her.

I sat on the ground next to where we dug the grave, atop some unsettled dirt that had formed into little mounds. I leveled one and rotated my bottom to a comfortable position. My hand drew slowly across the place I thought her face might be, then down to her heart. With my hand sitting softly upon the dirt, I cried my goodbye. "Mama."

The Day I Saw the Hummingbird

I waited for the thoughts to come, but all that came were feelings: painful memories of her last hours on this earth, the struggle she was put through and all that she had to endure. *Why? Because our skin is dark?*

I recalled her soothing me after Pursey's hanging, when there was some nasty mention of *that black man deserved it.*

"Why," I asked Mama, "did he deserve it 'cause he was black?"

"No explaining that, son. We got red blood like everybody else. We every bit a person as the next. Don't you be forgetting that."

"But—"

"But nothing! Skin color don't make us no less a person. Anybody says so be talking evil words of hate." She looked deep into my eyes, penetrating my sad soul. I felt her love infusing my limbs, climbing up to my shoulders, chest, insides, permeating my entire body.

I looked at Mama's grave and felt her saying, *If anyone ever say you ain't a human being, whole and good, don't you believe it. Not for one minute!*

I knew Mama was right. If I was going to get to freedom safely, Mama and her lessons to me about keeping a level head and following the goodness in my heart were the reasons.

I don't remember how long I sat outside under the cloud-covered moon. As the waves of shadows moved along my line of vision, my memories changed and shifted. Laughing with Mama, working beside her, waking to her weary snoring sounds, watching her prepare meals, smelling her good cooking, and paying attention when there was something serious she needed me to understand. One the most important things she told me was that we are known by how we make someone else feel. We may not remember the words that were said to us or the objects that were given to us, but we sure remember how they made us feel. *Be good. Be kind. Don't never let anger tempt you. It do you no good to hurt another* she told me frequently. She lived those words. I wasn't so sure I'd be able to follow in her footsteps, though. There were too many times I wanted to lash out and do harm to Prescott and his men. I could have killed them all. I didn't even try because I knew Mama would've been punished right along with me and I'd never let that happen. *But what was stopping me now, now that she was dead?*

The Day I Saw the Hummingbird

I didn't want to dwell on such bad thoughts that last time I sat at her burial place. Instead, I thought of the good times we had: her holding my hand as we walked out to the fields, the way she tended to me day and night when I was sick, the special meals she made when Macy brought leftovers from the main house, the hugs and back rubs when I couldn't sleep, and the laughter. I loved the sound of her laughter. And singing in the morning while fixing breakfast. She made up the silliest songs! The crisp night air upon my skin felt warmed as I continued to remember many past times with her.

On the next day, Sunday, we worked until noon. When we came back, Sammy and I hung around with Kitch and Albert. We wondered where Macy was until we spotted her running up to us, wildly shaking her empty hands. When I saw she hadn't brought us any food, a rock felt like it was forming in my belly. In a lowered tone, she frantically told us that she had heard something about a runaway who was drawn and hanged.

The day was still warm and balmy. Albert held up a hand to hush what she was saying. Motioning to the door of my place, he said. "It so hot out here. Can we go inside?" It was obvious to me that Albert was trying to get us away from any uninvited ears that might be listening.

Once in my cabin, I asked, "What's drawn?"

Macy shook her head indicating she had no idea.

Kitch knew what it meant. He took hold of my shoulder. His fingers tightened, and I flinched. He loosened his grip in an apology. "Sorry, Oscar." With a severe, solemn stare, he said," Drawn, oh, that a bad thing. A runaway get dragged by a horse." He cleared his throat.

Reflecting back to what Macy first said, I repeated, "Drawn *and* hanged. That's awful."

"It be that," said Kitch. "But before hanged, God only know what torture he get. No need my saying things I hear. Lots of things get passed around to scare slaves to thinking twice before fixin' to run. Dunno what be real or not. Heaven help us if half of what I done hear be true."

No further explanation was needed. We all looked at Macy, wiping sweat from her cheeks and neck, with those big eyes of hers open wide and looking like she'd just seen something ungodly.

"Mr. Coleson, he laughed when he mentioned a dirty nigger chained round the neck like a dog." She wiped her eyes, clearing away the overflowing tears, then told us that men in groups, called posses, were being paid to capture runaway slaves. Dead or alive. "The missus was upset 'bout all the violence that Mr. Coleson mentioned. It was hard to make out exactly what she was saying. Something 'bout...Oh, I dunno. It didn't make no sense to me. An eye for an eye and no one seeing nothing."

"Oh, no!" Sammy whispered. "Now what?"

Kitch responded, "Maybe best to wait?"

Albert nodded agreement. "It sound too dangerous, boys." He looked at Sammy and then at me.

Macy just sat there smacking her lips, making *tsk tsk* sounds.

My nerves got on edge from the sound of her tongue clapping the roof of her mouth. Nervously tapping my foot, I remembered sitting by Mama's gravesite last night and the conversation I had in my head. I took a deep breath and said, "We go. If we wait till a safe time, be old men. We go now."

Sammy's head jerked in my direction. "You sure?"

I knew by his grin that he wasn't asking a question. Maybe he asked for the benefit of the others, to make it seem as if we were giving the plan a little more thought. But we didn't need any more thinking. We had thought this through until our heads hurt. There would be no staying with Prescott and his band of monsters. No way were we sticking around. Go and die trying would be a better option than continuing the misery we knew. In a whisper, I said to the three friends we'd be leaving behind, "We gonna go." They all looked on, waiting for what came next. The moment of silence we shared was deep and heartfelt, a loving kinship. "We still young enough to try to make our lives better. By the sounds of it, the longer we wait, the harder it gonna be to get outta here." I knew the expression on my face must have reflected the same sorrow I saw on theirs.

There was no further disagreement, no protests or attempts to change our minds. Sammy's widening smile and fist thrust forward let me know that he was right in there with me.

Albert finally asked, "What time?"

"Probably round midnight," I replied.

We'd wait until the moon had been out for a while and the crickets brought nighttime sounds. I knew the sounds that came out when the sun had long been down. It was never entirely quiet where we lived near the fields. Night sounds were different than day sounds. Not all animals slept during the night.

Not all slaves wanting to be free did either.

The Day I Saw the Hummingbird

Chapter Twenty-One

I tried to rest. Lying on my mattress, my mind wouldn't stop. But I needed it to stop so I could get some sleep. We'd be traveling all night, and I needed my strength. I wondered how Sammy was getting on. I assumed the same as me. I tried to still myself by concentrating on pleasant things: flowers, the sun breaking through on a cold day, learning new words, and throwing rocks with Sammy. When the patter of footsteps and the low hum of conversations quieted, I waited. I continued to wait until a night owl hooted and yelped. When it whistled its song, I knew it was time. I went to the door and listened for Sammy's approach.

Several minutes passed.

All I heard was the owl's rhythmic beak snapping.

And then a loud *k-r-r-r-r-ick*.

It reminded me of another night a while ago when I was unable to sleep and I went outside. There, by the light of a bright moon, an owl was perched up a tree. With an upright stance, large wide head, eyes focused together, and big sharp claws encircling a limb, its attention was focused on something I couldn't see. I wondered what it saw. When its head rotated and it rapidly swooped down, I had my answer. It caught a small rodent. That owl could hunt. I could learn from it—the way it waited patiently, and, when it was sure of success, it acted precisely and exactly.

Sammy walked in and disrupted my thoughts. He knew not to knock. And like the owl in its quiet contemplation of what it needed to do to survive, we began our journey among the animals of the night.

When Sammy held a finger to his lips, indicating it was no talking from here on out until we reached a safe place, I got a bad case of nerves. I took a deep breath as we listened for danger for several very long minutes. Absent footsteps, dog sounds, or any strange noise, I hoped that wherever Prescott was, he was passed out drunk. I braced myself while envisioning Buddy. *Please let him be out of earshot.*

I nodded toward the door. I was ready.

We tiptoed out. The longest exit of my life moved by painfully slowly. The moon's glow was blocked by clouds and the shadows on the ground made it hard for us to see where to step. Each footstep brought the frightening possibility that we might land on a noisy leaf or twig and be discovered.

We didn't make a sound loud enough to wake anyone interested in stopping us.

Finally, we were out beyond the slave quarters and sugarcane fields. We were out of hearing-distance from the dangers we had miraculously left behind.

Now we faced new risks.

I had often wondered what it would feel like to be away from the plantation. What would freedom feel like? So far, freedom felt like being a hunted animal. Hyper-alert, the only thing that existed for me was what my eyes could see, my ears could hear, and any unusual smells that could alert me to peril—a campfire, soldiers, or dangerous creatures of the night. My hand reached for Sammy's back. I needed the security of contact. Just the feel of Sammy's body slightly lessened my queasiness.

Worried we might be headed in the wrong direction, I reminded myself of something Kitch had told us. "You start heading out thataway." He had pointed east. "Set your eyes on them eastern stars." His finger had moved to the sky in the direction he'd indicated then shifted position. "Next head toward them northern stars. They gonna guide you home."

Home. The sound of that word was sweet music to my ears. I didn't know where that would be. But I trusted that as long as I was free, home would be better than the only one I'd know so far.

Sammy continued to lead the way, with me never far behind. Trudging on, we put one foot in front of other slowly and deliberately until we heard the rush of water. Its coolness caressed my cheek. We wanted to find a shallow place to cross to erase our scent from any dogs that may be on our trail. When a group of clouds floated by and let the moon's light shine, we saw our opportunity. It was a narrow passage with large rocks jutting above the stream. Hoping that was an indication it was shallow, we made our way. It was hard to hold my sack and food pouch above my head while balancing on those rocks, but I'd strain until the end of time if I had to, just to keep on going. The water rose to my knees. I moved forward. Sammy was a good two feet in front. Halfway across, I saw that he hadn't sunk any deeper. I breathed easier.

When we reached the other side in dripping pants and squeaking shoes, we found a tall tree with a wide trunk and hid behind it. Sammy raised and lowered his hand, motioning for us to sit and stay there. I slid off my shoes. Then took off my pants and socks, wrung them out, and hung them on a tree branch to dry. I picked up a couple of dry leaves to clean my cold, slimy legs. I grabbed another garment out of my bag to cover myself with.

My worries settled into my head as I sat there. *Is we safe just sitting here? Ain't we better off moving? If one of them posses be hunting us, ain't they gonna catch up quicker?* But, I was exhausted and didn't want to keep going.

Sammy finished undressing and leaned over to me, his lips near my ear. He whispered, "We out for a good while. See the moon?" He looked up at the sky, "Daylight coming fore too long."

Sure enough, we watched the moon tuck below the trees and the sky start to get lighter. A few birds drifted by. It looked to be a warm, clear day.

"We gonna just stay here today?" I asked.

"I reckon it be best to stay put. We been lucky," he said in a low voice. "Sundown come in another twelve hours. Then we have a good hunk of travel time."

I patted his hand, signaling my agreement. We both wanted to keep talk down to a minimum. I was exhausted from no rest the night before and too many other recent nights of tossing and turning. I shut my weary eyes and drifted off.

Just when I felt the comfort of a sound sleep, a loud swishing woke me. It was a group of alligators, maybe four or five, rising out of the water. I held myself tightly and tried not moving a muscle as I watched them glide by. As gently as I could, I poked Sammy. He startled, opened his eyes and gave me a raised-forehead, alarmed look. When I pointed to the water, the expression on his face eased. He must have thought I had heard soldiers and was relieved to see a bunch of hungry alligators. As I stared at the large, broad-snouted, black colored predators, I wasn't as relaxed as Sammy appeared to be. When one of them opened its mouth, I slid back a foot. I'd never seen so many sharp teeth in my entire life. I didn't even know that many teeth could fit into a mouth. There musta been over fifty. *Keep going. Don't be looking at us!* I held onto a lungful of air until they all passed. Exhaling, I lowered my head back down near Sammy's. "I woke you 'cause I didn't know what they'd do."

"I figured. Sure done scared me good." His cheek twitched. "Thought for sure we got caught." He rubbed the spot where his face was fluttering "You hungry?"

"Sure am, what you got?"

He had about the same thing I had. We decided that it was best to ration the food. That afternoon we ate uncooked yams with water.

We spent the rest of the day by that sheltering tree. I busied myself thinking about the good folk who were against slavery. The ones who were going to open their homes to help us. Kitch had mentioned that the conductor man from his other plantation told him about these places that gave runaway slaves food and protection. Even money. There were a lot of routes from the South to the North, he told us. He also shared what he knew about the woman named Harriet, a former slave herself, who helped many slaves make it to freedom. Every time I heard that woman's name, I got a warm feeling in my chest. Just thinking there were decent, heroic people out there helping us gave me hope. Remembering what Kitch told us about the way to know if the house was safe also relieved my mind. Owners notified runaways with brightly lit candles in their windows or lanterns in front of their houses.

With Mama gone and the knowledge that so many kind-hearted people lived to help other human beings, my desire for freedom strengthened. The spark that had formed in the first planning talks while Mama was alive had grown into a powerful yearning. Having Sammy with me was a blessing. He was now my family. While Mama was alive, leaving would've been next to impossible. To say goodbye to her soft embrace and sad brown eyes was what I dreaded. With her gone, there was nothing holding me to that place. I often wondered about Kitch and his family. Although he never wanted to talk about them, the pain in his eyes said it all. I know he gave up his freedom in hopes of being reunited with them.

When the moon was edging up the night sky, we began traveling again. We headed east along waterways. Crossing meadows and passing over hills by dark, we were guided by the eastern stars. At daybreak, we rested in the forest. Sammy spotted some wild berries. It's funny how such simple things as wild berries can lift a person's spirits. At least for a little while.

Chapter Twenty-Two

The sight of berry juice dripping onto Sammy's chin made me laugh. Squeezing my lips together, I tried to suppress it. But the look on his face with that big pink tongue licking areas where the purple darkened his honey-brown skin sent me into fits of the giggles.

He threw himself at me and held my mouth shut.

"I can't breathe," I objected.

When he pressed harder, I dug my teeth into his palm.

"Ouch!" He instinctively pulled his hand back. "Stop it. Hush it down." If a whisper could be yelled, he did it.

"Couldn't help it." A last chuckle escaped. "Oh, if you ain't just a pretty sight. That purple…" I snorted a spray of mucus. Still clenching my jaw, I regained my composure. "Um. Sorry. You just funny."

Sammy wiped his face with the back of his arm. He looked at the muddy brownish-purple color I found so humorous. "That what funny?" He wasn't smiling. Shaking his head, he mumbled, "Just keep hushed."

I shrugged. "Sure look like you enjoy them berries." I made my way to the shrub with stems sprawling on the ground full of dark, almost black, berries. The thicket was crawling with little bugs eating its leaves. A few small beetle-like insects were having a meal of the berries. It reminded me of nights in bed with Mama asleep when I'd hear a creepy skittering sound. Remembering the feel of things crawling up my exposed limbs, I jerked and rubbed my arm. Now I had to get accustomed to things that had bothered me in the past. I had to learn to live among all the creatures on my journey toward freedom. I reached for the fruit and picked a bunch.

The nectar-filled, soft cluster tasted a little tart and earthy. The next mouthful, darker in color, was sweeter. As I continued to devour handfuls, my stomach growled. When I washed it down with a swig of water, the gurgling in my belly moved lower. Much lower. Severe cramping in my gut sent me running while doubled over. In a hidden area of covered bush, my bowels exploded. One bout and I felt relieved. Then the grumbling in my insides returned. I dropped my pants to go again. Out came liquid, solid particles, and a lot of wind. Just when I thought I was finished, another urge hit me. That was a sorry lesson in what eating too many wild, probably unripe, berries can do to the gut. After several more episodes, I wasn't about to raise my pants back up until I was sure I wouldn't soil myself. The brush that I tried to hide behind while squatting did little to block my sight. Through a small opening, I saw Sammy smiling in my direction as I continued to pass more air.

While waiting to be sure my insides had calmed down, I heard something. Narrowing my eyes into slits, I looked through that opening to see where the sound was coming from. Sammy was out in the open, exposed, while I was surrounded by the hands of welcoming limbs in the wilderness. There was nothing for me to do but stay put.

The sound became louder. It was footsteps.

Gooseflesh formed on my skin and a prickling sensation ran down my back. I wanted to yell for Sammy to run, but I kept quiet as he stood there frozen.

I moved a few inches away from the mess I made and lay down on the marsh. As my body molded with the soft ground, I kept motionless. Staring with desperate attention through a low-lying view, I saw the bushes in front of Sammy move. I bit my quivering lip, took a deep breath and watched as the foliage parted.

I nearly passed out from disbelief.

And relief.

To my utter amazement, two Negro men emerged from the shrubs, both looking as surprised as I felt. One of them frantically waved his arms and said something I couldn't make out. I grabbed several dry leaves, wiped myself, and pulled my pants back up. When I walked out to the clearing, they had a wide-eyed bewildered appearance.

The older and taller one was better dressed and didn't look like any slave I'd ever seen. He had on what seemed like new pants and a wool jacket. Although dirty from what must have been forest travel, his clothes looked brand-new, not like the hand-me-downs Sammy, me, and what his younger-looking companion had on.

The young one, Ned, was a slave. But the older one, Jackson, was a conductor escorting Ned to safety. Jackson was on his third trip. Kitch had told us about conductors. Good old Kitch.

At first, meeting a real live conductor for the Underground Railroad felt too good to be true, too unreal to be happening. How was it possible that Sammy and I were trying to find our own way to freedom and we just happened to run into someone experienced in leading escapees? If luck ever took notice of me, it wasn't the good kind. But there he was: a man who knew how to help us finish what we started.

After I came to my senses, I noticed that he seemed more agitated than surprised. Why? And why was he so frantic moments earlier?

Curious, I watched and waited. My answer came.

Jackson looked back to where they had just come from, then he turned to us. Droplets of sweat formed on his creased, worried-looking forehead. "A couple of days ago, we was followed." He slicked back his oily hair. That's when I noticed how smooth his hands looked. Not chapped, scrapped, worked, and dry like mine. What kind of life did a man with unworn hands have?

Concerned that they were still being followed and soldiers might be lying in wait, my heart moved into my throat.

"What you mean, 'followed'?" asked Sammy.

"A posse come after Ned. Probably sent by his plantation owner."

I looked at Ned. He wasn't a big man, and his slumped posture made him look even shorter. His sunken cheeks gave him a hungry look. And when I saw two big, thick scars on his face, I wondered what his life had been. "Just Ned?" I asked. "What 'bout you?"

"No, I was a house butler. Left that place a few months past on a faked sale to another plantation." That he worked in a main house, like Macy, explained his smooth hands. Ned remained silent as Jackson continued. He told us that he was assisted to freedom but returned to help others. Back in the South again, arrangements were made for him to assist Ned. "After traveling a couple days, we were hid in a valley surrounded by bramble and briar when a group came up on horseback. They was in earshot but we was hid good. I could see there was at least four of them."

I scratched the itch forming on my left arm spreading up to my armpit—my body telling I was too nervous (as if I needed reminding). I chewed a fingernail as I listened. The itching and worrying got worse.

"We stayed put till darkness come." Jackson took in a deep, slow breath and looked at Ned. "Not hearing nothing suspicious for several hours, we gambled it was safe and left. Pretty sure no one saw or followed us. Pretty sure."

Ned nodded agreement and finally spoke. "We not be free if they was on our tail."

"No dogs?" asked Sammy.

"None we saw or heard," replied Jackson.

I exhaled what I had been holding in. And feeling very insecure about our shaky situation, I tried to convince myself as much as anyone else when I said, "Sounds like you safe. Hope so, or we all in trouble." Fear floated in my belly as visions of being caught and hung stomped through my head. The image in my mind of vultures surrounding my dead body didn't help the itching now spreading to my other arm.

Sammy, more confidently said, "Ain't nobody here now. You probably safe."

Continuing to feel uneasy, I stuttered, "I think, um, we need...we should get a move on." I wanted to grab Sammy and get away from Jackson and Ned as fast as we could. My fear blocked rational thinking. I wasn't considering the fact that we were with a man who knew the trails and the locations of safe houses.

Sammy was more logical than me. He suggested, "How 'bout we all stay close together?"

When Sammy looked at me, my concentration was still on all the trouble we would be in if we were caught. And being caught was a good possibility since neither of us was experienced in escaping or surviving on our own.

Before I knew it, we were a four-man team. Four men were easier to spot than two. But Jackson convinced us that, if danger came, it would be handy to have extra muscle to fight or more to scatter in different directions increasing the chances that at least not all of us would get caught. We headed back into the thicket to pack our things and rest until nighttime. I went through the motions without protest.

About an hour until we began, Sammy asked Jackson how he got involved in helping runaways. "I worked on that there plantation I mentioned afore. The master, he a bad man. Breaking his rule brought down heavy punishment."

"Like what?" asked Sammy.

I wanted to kick him to make him be quiet. I had enough nightmares running through my head. Hearing Jackson telling us about slaves who were murdered was bad enough. Telling us that those who were killed mercifully were the *lucky* ones jolted me. The unlucky ones, he said, were mutilated. One man had a limb amputated. I shuddered at the thought of some poor innocent person having an arm or leg cut off. If he didn't bleed to death or die of infection, he'd spend the rest of his life being tortured for being a cripple.

Trying to veer the conversation back to why Jackson got involved in helping free slaves and away from the horrors of slave treatment, I gently steered us back with my question. "How'd you come to conducting? That's what they call you, ain't it? A conductor?"

"Yes." He took off his hat and wiped his brow. "A Negro woman helping musta heard 'bout how mean our master was. She got word to a group of us 'bout escaping if we want to."

"How?" I asked.

"She worked with white folk and other free Negroes. Dunno how they get information to us. Come to me secondhand. They fix up the plans. Not everyone feel safe leaving. Most too scared of torture. Me, I had enough. I wanted out. My family, they was all dead..." He lowered his head. "Dunno how she done it, but she had a white man come offering money up to buy him a couple of slaves. Not working the field, the master musta reckoned he could best do without me."

We all sat and waited, giving him time to sort out what was brewing inside. Grief and anger. I knew the feelings and the way they showed themselves too well: slumped shoulders, tears, and the way he kept pounding his right fist into his opened left palm.

He took a cloth out of his pocket and wiped his eyes. "I got freed by the help of that there woman and her friends."

"Why you come back after you got free?" asked Sammy.

"Strange thing. I reckoned free means free, but it don't. Least not to me. Sleep wouldn't come at night with all my thinking of what was happening to my people I left behind. I lost my family, but I still had friends. I was lucky to get help and I wanted to be spreading some of my good luck round to other folk. So, I joined the movement. First time I get me a man through to the North, well, ole Jackson sleep good that night! Not much more a man can want is a good night sleep, ain't that a fact?"

"But it so dangerous," said Sammy.

"Sure, but what kinda life did I have feeling all miserable inside for not doing nothing to help them poor souls still fighting for their lives?"

Somehow, I understood. Jackson, just like me, didn't have much to lose. And what was life without relationships: family we're born to and family not of our blood but of forged bonds. With every word that came from him, my comfort level increased. Good thing because my arms were beginning to turn raw from scratching. There was another thing I was curious about. "You know the name of the Negro lady that helped you?"

"Harriet."

There was that name again. The mysterious name that started it all. I asked more questions and found out from Jackson that she had guided many slaves out, including her family members. She was working with many abolitionists. There were good people out there laboring to free slaves.

As the heat of the sun was diminishing and the light was growing dimmer, I continued to listen. What I heard convinced me that Sammy and Jackson were right in suggesting we all stay together.

When the time was fitting, the four of us headed out. My feet sunk in the marsh and the mud clung to my shoes like an enemy holding me back. When Jackson extended a helping hand, it gave me resolve to keep on moving.

Chapter Twenty-Three

Jackson, a man bursting with information, reminded me of Kitch. Both were men that kept their eyes open and ears tuned to what was happening around them. Since Jackson was purchased and got connected with people helping slaves, he had learned about the Fugitive Slave Act. It was an actual law of the land. Slave owners never took kindly to their slaves up and leaving any more than they liked having their livestock wandering off or getting poached. So, they made sure that the law was on their side when it came to their property. Make no mistake, slaves were their property. The war between the states changed many things, and one of them was the enforcement of the Fugitive Slave Act. It got stricter, making life more dangerous for anyone who violated it.

Jackson told us that, by law, captured slaves had to be returned to their masters, and free states had to cooperate. Hearing this, I questioned whether we'd ever make it beyond the forest. Even if we did, then what? I had to keep telling myself that the only thing to do was continue north and face whatever came. Trying to convince myself that everything would turn out fine was like swallowing an onion. Whole.

Jackson was in the lead as we moved along in single file. He had told us that the first safe house we'd stop at was a little over a day away. If we didn't have to stop and stay put for any reason, that meant two more nights of travel before we arrived. Looking up at the moon, I was glad for the nearly-full light it cast. There were times that came before when a light in the dark soothed my fears, particularly in bed when scampering things crawled nearby. Remembering the sound of scurrying coming from the walls and roof of our cabin on the Coleson Plantation, I wiggled my back to relieve a fidgety discomfort. It felt like a premonition when Jackson held up a hand to stop us and nodded toward a pair of glowing eyes frozen near a bush. Before it had a chance to flee, Jackson threw a knife pinning it to the ground. It was a big rodent. Had its eyes not reflected the glow from the moon, we probably would have missed it.

Grabbing the hilt of his knife, Jackson whispered, "Look like we got us some fresh meat to eat."

The Day I Saw the Hummingbird

He lifted the limp, furry thing and passed it closer for us to see. Gritting my teeth, sickness rose up my chest and spit slid down the sides of my mouth. I was disgusted to think of eating a rodent that we just killed. What Kitch had taught us was being put to the test. My stomach churned, and I closed my lips real tight in squeamish protest.

Jackson must've seen my reaction. He blew out air through his nose in a silent laugh and directed his comment at me, "That meat ain't bad. Got protein. Good for you."

"Protein?" Another new word to remember.

"Animal meat," Jackson replied. "Different from plants, fruits, and vegetables." He grabbed hold of the carcass with his left hand and removed the knife with his right.

As I watched him begin to skin the animal, my squeamishness turned to wonder. How did he know so much? I wanted that ability. He was skillful with his cutting. First, he chopped off the head, then the legs, and, lastly, opened the belly to take out the insides. The sight of its innards with blood oozing out relieved me of my growing hunger.

"You see its lit-up eyes?" Jackson finished the task and continued, "I seen it in alligators." He gathered some twigs into a pile, rubbed two together for a long time and made a small fire.

I paid attention to any noises that may indicate that our small fire or the smell of the smoke was noticed by anyone in close enough range. It was hard to concentrate on anything else.

Sammy appeared quite interested in what Jackson had to say. He added, "I seen animals that don't do that. They eyes is dull. How come?"

"We all different. Guess there something in some eyes that make a glow."

I remained quiet along with Ned. When the dead thing was cooked, Jackson buried the last of the flames and embers by dousing the smoke in dirt. He waited a couple minutes for our meal to cool. When it was ready to eat, he handed a section to Sammy. Then he turned to face me. I picked it up between my thumb and first finger like some slimy thing I wanted to throw away.

Sammy ate his piece, looked at me and shook his head. "Ain't gonna bite you, Oscar. *You* gotta bite *it*! Can't hurt you now."

The Day I Saw the Hummingbird

The first chomp was tough to break off and caught in the space between my front teeth. I worked it loose and chewed on it until I swallowed the lump. Getting that first piece down wasn't easy. The next few mouthfuls were easier. I was able to get sense of the flavor; it tasted like old, gamey chicken.

Once we finished eating, we continued on with our nighttime trek. As daylight began to surface, we settled in by a wide stream. I wanted to clean myself before dawn fully broke. Sammy and Ned, too exhausted to want to do anything but rest, stayed behind under a tree in a relatively covered hiding area. Jackson came along with me. We undressed and left our clothes under a bush at the water's edge. We checked for gators.

Submerging my body into the cold drink was refreshing. Smiling at myself for making such a fuss earlier, I washed the dinner drippings from my hands and arms. I watched Jackson drift on his back and wondered how he stayed above the water. He dipped all the way under then up he came, his large body splashing a couple-foot spray. Except for the ripples we made, the water was calm. Still feeling the bottom with my feet, I moved closer to Jackson. Suddenly, I lost my footing and was completely plunged in a muddy, swirling mess.

I panicked.

Flailing my arms, I tried to resurface.

I was still under. No air. *I don't wanna die like this!*

Just as I imagined my doom, I felt Jackson's arms around my waist lifting me to fresh air. A forced deep breath made me cough. He moved me back to where I could stand.

"You're good." He squinted at the sun rising in the east. "Don't you go scaring me like that again. I'm in the business of freeing folk, not watching them drown." He smiled.

I was still feeling shaky, and I wanted to get out of that water. Fast.

His brows knitted together to avoid the sun's glare. "I can show you swimming." Hesitating, he looked toward where Sammy and Ned were sleeping, and tilted his head like he heard something. His eyes moved to the bushes separating them from us, blocking a clear line of sight. As there was just silence and it seemed like it was nothing, he continued. "There ain't much of trick to not sinking. Wanna learn?"

I was afraid to try. Afraid I'd go under again and he wouldn't be able to save me. But being scared had become a way of life. It hadn't stopped my actions, but it made me feel awfully nervous while carrying on in the path of danger. Once again, my head was active with thoughts—way too active—and ventured down dangerous paths when no threats were present. I looked into his undistracted, sincere face and saw a friend. I opted to trust him. "Sure," I muttered.

"Here," he said, taking my hands in his, "lemme grab ahold of you and you straighten up your body."

I did as he instructed, but my legs sunk. Hopeless. When I started to remove my grip from his hands, he grabbed tighter. "Straighten them legs out behind you and kick under the water. Just enough to move. Not enough to make a splashing sound."

I remembered how he did it. First one foot then the other.

"Good, real good," he smiled. "Now, move faster."

I did. *I did it!* And I stayed on top of the water. As he started to let go of my arms to show me how to move them, I lost the motion. My feet were back on the bottom. I watched him make wide arm strokes. I made the same movements. It felt good. Liberating. Combining the arm and leg motion, he floated off, and then returned to me. "Go on, you try."

After several attempts, I moved further into the deeper water, where moments before I thought I was going to drown. The minutes passed and I relaxed into the movement. This was the first time I'd ever been swimming. I liked how it felt. I felt free.

Suddenly, he waded back to a shallow area next to the bank protected by overhanging bushes. Ankle-deep in the water, he looked around like he did before the swimming lesson began. He motioned for me to come to him. His finger over his mouth was a signal I knew well. *Be as quiet as possible.*

I made it back to Jackson quickly and quietly. That's when I heard what he must have heard: noise coming from the direction where Sammy and Ned were. We slipped out of the water to where our clothes were. He picked up all our things and moved to an area thick with brush. I followed and got down on my belly next to him.

I had a sinking feeling that I wouldn't be getting much rest that day.

Chapter Twenty-Four

The sound of a breaking branch was followed by an eerie silence.

For several seconds, I heard nothing but Jackson's breath.

Just as I dared to breathe, more tree limbs snapped and dry leaves cracked.

Then I heard the horse hooves.

Next, all hell broke loose.

Unintelligible screams started coming from where Sammy and Ned should have been. My bladder emptied onto the ground beneath me. Unable to stop my legs from shaking, I grabbed onto the earth I was clinging to. Jackson up against me, as still as prey avoiding a predator, raised high enough to peek through the shrubs.

I turned my neck to get more air in through my nose. When I did, Jackson gave me a look that needed no interpretation: *keep your head down and be quiet.* Mama gave me that look many a time.

The shouting grew louder. "We got 'em!" A gruff voice bellowed.

Another gravelly roar sent shivers up and down my body. "There's that nigger."

Not a word from Sammy or Ned.

I prayed they weren't dead. I wished Jackson would do something. Tell me something.

When the first voice yelled, "Get the rope round that boy's neck," I felt an odd kind of relief. *They still alive. There still time to help them.*

Cringing, I wondered how long it would take for the strangers to find us. But the commotion continued without them getting close to us. They didn't seem to know we were hiding in the tall brush.

Then I heard a moan. I knew it was Sammy. I bit my lip to hold back the protests racing through my head. I wanted to stand and scream, "Stop this madness! Stop!" I wanted to run to Sammy and Ned to help them. I wanted to kill the bastards who I knew were torturing them. My anger took over. I made a move to get up. All I could think of was killing them, getting even for all the people who died unjustly. I'd seen enough!

Jackson grabbed hold of my arm and jerked me back down. His lips to my ear, he was forceful when he said, "You gonna get us killed! Stay put."

Hearing the moans from Sammy, I squirmed to release Jackson's grip, but he held me firm.

Again, he screamed a loud whisper into my ear. "You don't wanna die. I don't neither. Settle down."

Putting the fear back in me, he continued to hold onto me till I calmed down and lost the urge to lash out. My legs continued to tremble and tears streamed down my muddy cheeks as the noise intensified and what must have been a tree limb cracked. Then I heard a heavy thud, and more horse movement came before the man with the gruff voice screamed, "Get him back up there."

Sammy groaned again and cried out, "Pleeeease don't…" before a snapping sound gave way to sickening quiet.

"Get that other stupid nigger back to his master," yelled the last man who gave the orders. "Alive!"

My pounding heart was ready to burst as the horses' pounding hooves became a distant echo. Still afraid to get up, I refused to move when Jackson stirred and raised his head. I wanted to grab his full head of hair and yank him back down. My aching fingers stretched out in the attempted effort, but my hand wouldn't move. Frozen in terror, anger, and too many overwhelming emotions all jumbled and confused, I felt Jackson's body move away from mine.

"Oh, dear Lord," he muttered. He got back down beside me. "Oscar, sit up. They gone."

His hand was on my naked back. I looked at his red eyes. "What happened?" I mumbled.

"I gonna tell you what I seen. To prepare you. But don't you say a word. Not nothing." He spoke softly. "Ain't sure they far enough away. If you yell or fuss, and they hear us—"

I jerked back from his touch and sat up. I had asked him what happened but I didn't want to hear more. I didn't want to know. I didn't want to fill my memories with more pain. The images of hatred inside of me were already overflowing and ready to burst.

"Listen up," he said in a serious, strained voice. "This ain't gonna be easy."

Finally, I'd had enough. My uncontrolled anger returned and surged at him. "What?" I screamed.

Keeping his voice down, he commanded me, "Pipe down!" Jackson wiped back hair that had fallen on his forehead; it stuck in a river of his own worry-sweat. "Sammy he dead. Hung from a tree."

"No!" I squealed. There they were, the words I dreaded, the confirmation of what I thought had happened. *No! No! No! No!* I silently, violently, shook my head back and forth feeling like I was going mad.

Abruptly, he grabbed hold of me and wrapped me up in his long, strong arms. "Shh," he whispered. "Stay quiet! Try to settle yourself." He held me tighter. "I knows how you feeling."

I believed him. It was something about the way he held me: his firm and compassionate warmth, a pervading sympathy in his tone. Yes, I believe Jackson *did* know how I felt. In that embrace, both of us without our clothes, I cried as if all the sorrows I ever felt ganged up on me and started whipping at my heart.

When I was drained dry of all my tears, I asked him, "What 'bout Ned?"

"They took him. Left a trail of blood and snapped branches. I figure they done horse-dragged poor ole Ned after beating him."

"Oh, no!" I shook my head. "Why?" My head ached so badly that I thought something had exploded in between my ears. I continued to whimper, "Why?" The only thing I could think of was that this was a posse that was hired to bring back Ned and mistook Sammy for the conductor. Those who helped a runaway were considered vermin to be squashed to death. And possessions, like us slaves, were property to be returned to their rightful owners. Everyone knew that.

Before I got up to see what was left of Sammy, I slowly put on my clothes. I didn't care that my skin was covered with mud. I didn't care if I smelled like a dead rat. I didn't care what the blazes I looked like. Dressed and braced for the worst, I moved to the clearing.

There was Sammy hanging from a tree, his head bent in an unnatural direction from the rope around his neck. Next to where he was slain, above his mangled bloated purple body, was a broken tree limb. On the ground beneath him was a large bowl-shaped area with the broken limb and one of his shoes. Knowing it was from the thud we heard earlier, I envisioned those crazy, hate-filled men stringing Sammy up not once, but twice.

Feeling sick to my stomach, I softly spoke to what was left of my friend Sammy. "Sorry, Sammy. You done nothing in your whole short life to deserve this." I then started to move to him to get him off that tree. He deserved a proper burial.

Jackson, catching wind of what I was up to, stopped me. "Wait."

I paused, my back to him.

He continued. "We gotta leave him."

I turned around. With flaring nostrils, tears streaming out of my eyes, I snorted and stamped my foot. "No! He ain't staying like that."

Once again, Jackson responded with patience and understanding. "Listen up." He took a deep, long slow breath. "We move him and the next posse or soldier coming along will figure they best be looking for another set of runaways or folks kindly to them. They be happy to hunt more of us. Best we can do for poor ole Sammy here is moving on. Stay alive. Make to it freedom." And then he leaned into me and said something that I almost didn't hear because he spoke so softly. It was as if it was carried on a whisper. "I'm sorry."

He was right. It pained me, but he was absolutely right. We had to keep moving on as soon as night came. We had to stay alive.

We went about a mile downstream and hid. One of the hardest days of my life was hiding while I knew Sammy was hanging there for predators to find. In the quiet of waiting for the hours to pass, for the steamy day to move into night, I mourned my loss. Not just of Sammy. But Mama. And my papa. And Pursey. And all the poor innocents whose lives met the same fate. Everything had been taken from me. I doubted I'd ever see Kitch again. Or Albert and Macy. I had nothing left.

Despair moved with the blood pulsing through my body. Feeling very down, self-pity and an intense ache for Mama overcame me. I craved the comfort of her arms holding me, the reassurance of her tender expressions, and the guidance of her wisdom. Physically gone from my life, so much of her still remained. It was then that the pain in my chest made room for something else. Mama's words rang inside of me, into the places that needed to heal: *Keep at them words. Keep writing in the dirt. You write in dirt but you ain't never dirt. Keep that there heart in you clean, and you soul gonna lead you right. Don't never hang on to pain. You gotta carry on with a happy heart. Life be easier if you keep you eyes on what you got.* I'd never feel her hold me again, but at least Mama's wisdom was always with me. The heaviness in my limbs felt a little lighter.

So much had been taken from me yet so much remained. My Mama taught me what it was to receive and give love. Sammy taught me how to play. Kitch taught me how to learn. All these lessons remained within me. I had to believe that I would rise from feeling beat down. Jackson would now teach me how to survive and take me to freedom. I would have a life worth living and it would have purpose. It was then that I felt thankful I didn't do something stupid earlier by lashing out. I was glad Jackson held me down. I was glad Mama came back to life in me to help me see that acting on despair, anger, and hatred just gets you more despair, anger, and hatred.

Oddly, I recalled that nasty voice yelling at poor Ned, "stupid nigger." I decided then that I wasn't going to be stupid or ignorant. And I would refuse to believe it if someone insulted my intelligence. Believing it would bring shame to me and everyone who loved and helped me find my way to freedom. Even in my agonizing grief, a beacon of hopeful light broke through the shadows: my first teacher, Kitch. Were it not for him and words written in the dirt, I would have never appreciated the gift I was given. He taught me more than words; he opened up a whole new world for me. The world of learning where a mind is free to explore just about everything. I never knew such a world existed. And I sure didn't know that kind of freedom was possible. Most folk like me are never given that opportunity. Most don't have a Kitch. I have

him to thank for lighting a fire in me. Remembering him
and his big toothless smile lifted me out of my self-pity.

Chapter Twenty-Five

That evening, we continued traveling until the brink of dawn. As light spread over the horizon, we hid deep in the backwoods surrounded by bramble, briar, and brush. Jackson slept soundly a few feet from me, but I had trouble falling asleep. The sorrowful thoughts keeping me awake were interrupted by the sound of two chipmunks harvesting and hoarding tree seeds in their burrows. Squinting my eyes, I got a closer look at the tan and black stripes running along their backs. I remained very still so as not to disturb their work. I had never paid much attention to forest critters. Now, I found them fascinating. I never knew a chipmunk's tail was longer than its body. Hairier, too. Their single-minded scurrying to grab food to store for the winter had me spellbound. Just as one lone chipmunk was transporting what looked like a piece of mushroom growing on the side of a tree, it stopped. Standing erect, it looked from side to side. I wondered if it sensed me watching it. When its head turned upward, I saw the reason for its concern. A hawk was perched on top of a tree. Its sharp, curved beak was pointed downward. Its wings spread for flight. A dark band across its tail showed as its talons loosened their grip. Down it swooped. It reminded me of the owl I once saw catching a rodent.

My gut twisted as the red-tailed hawk clamped onto the chipmunk, tightened its grasp and flew off with the animal struggling, no doubt, to its death. I felt no relief knowing it was a meal for the bird. I felt sorry for the poor chipmunk and hoped it didn't suffer.

I thought of Sammy and broke into tears. Opposing emotions were tormenting me. I wanted to live, to be freed and to find a good purpose in life. But I was also fighting the impulse to punish those (and the ones like them) who did harm to my family and friends. I couldn't help wavering. My fluctuating emotions felt as deep inside of me as my beating heart. Finding no way to control the pain that kept surfacing, I thought of that chipmunk. Hard working and industrious. And I thought of the lethal hawk. Each reminded me that, although I may not be able to control what comes up inside my head—or what spurs it on—I could do something about deciding my course in life. I related to that chipmunk and found it very unfair that keeping my head down, keeping quiet, and minding my own business gained no reward in a world where the ones with power could just swoop down and take everything away. Since I wasn't born a hawk, I'd somehow have to find a way to live with injustice and carry on.

Tossing and turning, I got no sound sleep before we began the next part of our trek.

* * *

How our lives end up on the paths we take is a mystery to me. Were it not for the day I saw the hummingbird, I don't know that I would have left. Sure, I planned on it. But deep down, I had a powerful urge to stay with Mama. With her gone, I was sadly set free. The pain of that freedom was a jagged stone to swallow, but some good came of it. I like to think that in some ways, in my early days out there on my journey to freedom, I gained the courage to be the man my mama wanted me to be. Being pushed out into the woods, as scary as it was, opened me up to new things. And in opening myself up, I found out that what I conjured up inside my head was often more frightening than what really lived in the world or among the creatures of the forest. I learned that most things aren't what I think they'll be. I learned that opportunity, not just danger, lies around every bend in the road—you just have to be on the road to find them.

One of those opportunities came shortly after the horrible incident with Sammy and Ned. The sorrow I carried about losing them and the fear that it could easily have been *me* eased when I met Maxwell and Sarah Whitfield. They were the owners of the first safe house Jackson and I stopped at. They were my first white friends. The first time I laid eyes on them was at a door at the back of their home.

Jackson and I arrived several hours after darkness on the second night after we left Sammy. Jackson had been there before and knew what to do. He lightly tapped the door in a rhythm that was arranged beforehand.

Knock, knock. Pause. Knock, knock, knock. Pause.

He repeated that two more times until Mr. Whitfield answered. He was wearing dark black pants and a clean blue shirt covered by a dark vest. The missus, behind him, instantly held out an arm to usher us in while he spoke. "Follow me," he nodded to Jackson.

Once we were all inside and the door was secured, the missus warmly smiled and said, "Welcome to our home. We'll get you settled in, then I'll bring you some food."

Sarah Whitfield reminded me of Mrs. Coleson. Both white women were kind to me. But that's where the similarity ended. Mrs. Whitfield was a colorful person, all lit up with a personality the likes of which I'd never encountered until then, nor since. Bubbly and genuine, she had a face filled with expressions. When she turned up her ruby-red lips in a contagious smile, her eyes turned from dark to bright green. Her cheeks bore a muted frost of pink and her small nose curved up like a curly, thin tendril of a planted vine. She wore a cheerful blue, full-bodice dress and decorated her ears with tiny dangling pieces of fine jewelry. Understated in speech, she was overly affectionate in gesture.

Her husband was a conservative, friendly fellow. Everything about him—his clothes, his carefully chosen words, his deliberate movements—told me he was a cautious man. But when he addressed me, he smiled generously, like the missus. Both were obviously passionate about their abolitionist activity. They put themselves in grave danger to help strangers. I never knew people like that existed. And I never forgot them.

The back entrance to their house led to the stairs that went down to the basement. In a small alcove, Mrs. Whitfield turned to face us and lowered her eyes to mine. "We're going to bring you downstairs to where you will hide." It's where they kept the runaways. Safe under the wooden floorboards and out of sight.

She looked to her husband, who continued to explain. "Jackson already knows the routine, but we'll review it to be sure you're kept safe." He put his hand gently on my arm. Wetness formed in his eyes when he said, "We're glad you're here."

The missus lowered her chin in agreement. Then she clapped her hands together as if trying to lighten the mood. "Come now, let's get you to safety."

Safety. Oh, how wonderful that word sounded coming from her honey-smooth voice. It made me feel warm inside. For the first time in two days, I smiled. I was fascinated by how they interacted with each other. Her sociable personality and his more discreet temperament seemed a perfect match. Like a seesaw, they balanced each other out.

Down in the dark, bare cellar, Mr. Whitfield lit a candle. I quickly glanced around to notice some scattered tools, two suitcases, and several storage boxes. The space was about 600-square-feet and smelled musty. The floor was made of planks. In the middle was an old wool carpet. The missus pointed to the rug. "You'll be safe there."

I wasn't sure where *there* was until Mr. Whitfield bent over, folded the carpet, and opened a lid on the floor. To look at it, you couldn't tell it was a hiding place. But once his fingers raised the slightly higher ledge, the separation of floorboards was evident. My new home was a crawlspace a little over four-feet high and as wide and long as the entire cellar. Since I was only slightly taller than that, staying down there wouldn't be a problem for me, but Jackson was much taller.

"I'm afraid you'll have to bend to move around down there," said the missus.

I just about cried when she apologized to us for the inconvenience. That simple act of kindness was a new experience for me. A new beginning. I had had valuable lessons before: reading, writing, and surviving in the forest. Now I was beginning to learn how to trust folks different than me. It was the first in a long series of events where I discovered firsthand that people of lighter color than me were just as kind as my mama and friends. I was overwhelmed with relief when I realized that people are people. Simple as that. And the color of my skin doesn't make me less of a person. It doesn't separate or define my humanness. No, what makes some less human is hatred and hateful actions.

Jackson and I settled into the crawlspace. There were four mattresses side-by-side, a couple of buckets for peeing and such, a wooden box turned upside down holding a bowl with some cold water in it for washing up, and a pitcher with more water for drinking. There were also two candles with matches that Mr. Whitfield left for us. The only other light would come through the cracks in the walls, also made of wood. The thick carpet covering some of the dirt floor intensified my feeling we were being housed by really kind folk.

Jackson instructed, "You hear footsteps, blow out them lit candles."

"Why?" I felt so safe in the Whitfield's house that I couldn't understand Jackson's worry.

"Might not be friendly feet. Don't want wrong eyes seeing through floor holes. And, we gotta put the flames out before sleep so we ain't starting no fires." He reached a hand to the wall and moved his fingers along the wooden surface. "Last I remember, there was some cracks in this here wall. Best make sure we got no lit candles after nightfall so nothing shine out and look strange. Folk can't see candle light outside in the day time." He told me that a lot of cellars were built underground but that this one was above ground. He had heard from Mr. Whitfield a couple of trips before that the plans to build this house included space to help slaves escape.

I was near speechless that the Whitfields had gone to so much trouble to help slaves. "Oh, my! They is good folk."

Smiling at me, he responded, "They wonderful folk, Oscar."

I smiled back at him. *Why they wanna help so much?* Before long I'd have my answer.

Soon there was a tapping above us. The same sound Jackson made at the back door. He whispered to me, "Food."

Sure enough, the missus returned with a plate of cornbread and pot of warm soup with two bowls and spoons. The soup was filled with lots of rice and vegetables. When I drank a mouthful of the tasty liquid, memories of Mama filled me up. But none of her soup had so many pieces of okra, peas, corn, and leafy mandingo. I swear that cornbread with honey came right from Heaven. Bite after bite, slurp after slurp, I filled my belly—and my soul—with gratitude.

That night was the first good sleep I'd had since my mama's death. I settled in to the familiar sound of Jackson's snoring. It was a comforting sound. Mama snored. I pretended she was by my side and fell fast asleep.

Upon awakening the next morning, I felt disoriented. It was daytime, but the space was mostly dark except for a few small cracks in the wall casting a tiny bit of light onto where Jackson was still asleep. Squinting my eyes, I peered through a small outside opening. The foliage looked the same as the places we had hunkered down in while on the run in the forest. But I saw more flowers in bloom in the Whitfield's yard. Purple clusters, pink bouquets, red spiking vine-like groups, and bunches of small white blossoms. As I admired nature's display, I wondered where we were. My attention was disrupted by a yawn coming from Jackson, who was rubbing sleep from his eyes.

There had been so much turmoil and disruption up until now that I hadn't thought to ask where we were. Feeling safe and comfortable, my suppressed curiosity sprang back to life. "Where we at?" I asked.

"Southwest Mississippi."

Jackson told me that we had walked from the lower part of Louisiana east to a marshy waterway. I assumed it was a route used by many runaways with conductors, as there were two rafts by the shore. My stomach jumped the entire time it took to get to the other side. Once there, we crossed into Mississippi. I couldn't tell you how many total miles we had trudged but, I figured that it was a long, harsh distance (if my feet were telling the story). I felt down to my bare swollen feet to rub loose the pain from stepping on jagged rocks and rough surfaces. My perspiring skin felt very warm to the touch.

"Mississippi sits east of Louisiana," he said.

I remembered directions from Kitch's map and also from conversations. It was in the direction of the big ocean, the East Coast. "Where we headed next?" I was very interested in the number of states involved in fighting for the South. The states fighting to keep slavery alive. I wondered where the dividing line was between the North and South and how long until we reached the land of liberation. I wondered if that place would feel any different than where I'd been.

Jackson reached for the candle and lit it. And like Kitch had done, he found a patch of dirt to draw a brief map. "Here," he pointed to several squares he had drawn together, one on top of the other moving in an easterly direction. "Right there." His index finger rested on the second box. "We here now. And…" I saw that Mississippi was to the side of where we'd come from. And above it a narrower square jutting to the right—again, easterly—was where he moved his finger next. "That there be Tennessee."

Impressed, I asked him, "How you know 'bout the states?" Without letting him finish, I said, "How come you know so much?"

Smiling, he responded. "Ain't hard to learn. Gotta open up your mind. Try things. Pay attention. Course, helps being a traveling man. I done learned—"

He was interrupted by the sound of footsteps above us. It was the missus with breakfast.

Chapter Twenty-Six

Mrs. Whitfield handed us steaming porridge alongside two pieces of thick toast and a cup of tea on a fancy platter. The look on the missus' face as she knelt down and passed the food to Jackson lingered in my head. Her worried, knitted-brow made me feel uneasy. It was a distinct change from her ease and friendliness last night. I didn't bring it up to Jackson, but it troubled me. Were we too much of a bother?

Concern dampened my appetite. So did the heat in the space we were occupying. Still wearing the clothes we had traveled in, I felt hot and sticky. I pulled my top away from my sweating chest to give it some air. Wiping droplets forming above my upper lip with the sleeve of my shirt, I asked, "You hot?"

"Hmm," he mumbled as he finished chewing a piece of toast. "Not really. Why?"

"I seems to be sweating up a storm." I remembered how warm my skin felt last night.

He reached the back of his hand to my forehead. "Feels like you has a fever. With all the goings on, I ain't surprised. Finish that meal and rest. By the time we gotta head outta here, I bettcha you gonna be fit as a fiddle."

"Yeah, suppose so." When I forced down a spoonful of cereal, my grumbling stomach threatened to bring it back up. I only ate a small portion of food then put my spoon down and pushed the plate away.

"Ain't hungry?" he asked, looking at my uneaten food.

Maybe I hadn't lost my appetite because of concern over Mrs. Whitfield's mood. Maybe now, in the safety of shelter, everything leading up to now was catching up with me. All I knew was that the heat and nausea building up in my body wasn't subsiding. And it hadn't eased off several hours later. After a nap, I awoke coughing and drenched in my sweat. I noticed that the tray of food was gone and so was Jackson. Alarmed, I sat upright.

Before I had time to work myself into a panic, I heard footsteps, and the trap door opened. Jackson had returned with Mrs. Whitfield. She bent to say, "We had an unfortunate event happen." She took in a deep, slow breath. "Jackson here," she put a hand on his shoulder and continued, "helped me with my husband." She went on to tell me that her husband was up on a ladder and lost his footing. When he landed on his right leg she heard a snap. Sure he'd broken a bone, she needed Jackson to help get him to his bed. She now wanted Jackson to deliver a message to get a doctor. Dangerous as it was, he agreed to help. Reminded of her earlier worried expression, I wondered if the accident happened before she brought our breakfast and she waited until after we ate to tell us. I must've been asleep when she returned to get Jackson's assistance.

"Need help?" I coughed a big blob of white mucus. And continued to have coughing fits until I brought up more mucus and cleared my airway.

Jackson quickly got down next to me and helped sit me upright.

"Don't be worrying over me," I protested, not wanting their attention on me while they had more important things to think about.

Jackson looked up to the missus then over to me. His lips were pinched tight as he shook his head. For a man who seemed to know about everything, he sure did appear at a loss for what to do.

"Go on. Help find a doctor for Mr. Whitfield. I'm good," I stubbornly insisted.

The missus nodded at Jackson. "Wait till dark. Then do what I told you. I'll take care of Oscar."

After nightfall, Jackson was gone.

Mrs. Whitfield was true to her word. Sitting on a wooden crate next to me, she cooled me with a wet cloth. She gave me tea and herbs, and I started to feel better. During one of her visits to me, she looked mighty frazzled. I asked again if there was anything I could do for her. With a warm, charitable smile she said, "You need to rest. Make sure you stay well. My husband is comfortable and he's happy I'm helping you."

Her kindness left me speechless. I just nodded and smiled.

She reached a comforting hand to my cheek. "You're so young." Her voice sounded wistful, soft and far away, like she was remembering a distant memory.

She pulled her arm away, but her touch lingered on my face. "I be ten-years-old soon enough."

"You seem older to me." A sudden tear dripped from her eye. "I had a son around your age. Zachary."

I didn't want to ask. I knew I shouldn't. Something had happened to her boy and whatever that something was, it hurt her. I knew that look all too well.

She wiped the wetness running down her chin. "I'm glad you made it this far, Oscar. I hope you make it all the way." She stood to leave.

"Missus," I called to her.

Before closing the trap door, she turned back to face me.

"Thank you, Ma'am."

Up moved those red lips of hers into a half-smile. She nodded, turned, and then she was gone.

A day passed, and Jackson had not returned. The meals came and went, along with light conversation. She told me they had family in New York City, her husband's brother and wife who were both teachers.

Upon hearing that they were teachers, I lit up. "I can write me some words. And read some too." I moved a part of the carpet to reveal some dirt. With my finger, I spelled O-S-C-A-R.

"That's wonderful," she said. Sitting there taking in my achievement, she grew pensive. After a minute or two, she asked, "Would you like me to teach you some new words?"

I was stunned. This fine woman had her whole house to tend to and a lame husband who needed looking after. I sure didn't want to impose any more than I already had just by being an extra mouth to feed. Not knowing what happened to her bubbly personality when she first opened her home to us weighed heavy on my mind, so I hesitated. I switched the question and asked her, "How Mr. Whitfield making out? Don't he need tending to?" I wondered if she was a little solemn because he had hurt himself. Or was it something else, something that shown in her face when she mentioned her son Zachary.

"Oh, him." She waved her hand as if shooing a fly. "As long as he stays still, he's not hurting and shouldn't make things worse for himself," she sighed. "He can hop around if need be…with help." She continued, "He's itching to get back on his feet, but I don't think that'll happen for a while. He won't like that, so I'll let the doctor give him that bit of news. Luckily, no other escapees have come through, and no posses have ventured out this way in a long time."

I got a pain in my chest when she said *posse*. "Has a posse ever come out here? Or soldiers?" I had to know.

"Only once, about a year ago. Two men wandered off their trail and landed here. It hasn't happened since. We're thick in the Mississippi forest." She told me that very few uninvited people ever came out through the thickets around there. But, she said, they still had to be very careful. When they decided that they wanted to help free slaves, the Whitfields (with the assistance of other abolitionist friends) built their home. It was situated far off normally used trails. That gave me a little better understanding of why they built the cellar above ground.

But where did the passion come from? Why were the Whitfields, and their friends, so passionate about helping us Negroes? How did it work, the Underground Railroad? What if Jackson didn't return? How would I know where to go? As if she read my thoughts, she shared with me that friends came from time to time on horseback with messages.

"Like what?"

"Oh, like when the next conductor would arrive with escaped slaves." She patted my hand. "Of course, sometimes unexpected surprises like Jackson and you just appear. And that's fine by us!"

If I didn't ask then, I don't know that I ever would have. "What get you to doing this?"

She hesitated for a long time. She shifted her position, too, from leaning in close to sitting straight and further away from me.

I don't think she wanted to answer me. But I waited her out.

Finally, she said, "It's just plain wrong to *own* another human being. A person is not property!"

Something had gotten to her, and it made her mad. That anger must be part of what motivated her to help. She wasn't willing to tell me just yet (if ever), but I sure understood how she felt.

***

Another day passed, and Jackson still hadn't returned. I hadn't brought up her offer to help me with spelling, but our conversations continued. I found out from Mrs. Whitfield that she was from a very wealthy southern family. Her mother had died while birthing her, and a Negro nanny raised her. Sarah Whitfield was an only child. When she was twelve, her nanny was out visiting her own family on their property when a drunken gang of no-goods came by and, in an intoxicated rage, beat up on several slaves. Mildred, her nanny, was killed. Mrs. Whitfield never got over that. She blamed slavery and the hatred of blacks for her loss. After her nanny's death, she vowed she would do what she could to help slaves and abolish slavery. When she was old enough, she met and married the man she fell in love with: Mr. Whitfield. He, too, was a passionate abolitionist. His whole family was involved in fighting slavery, including the brother she mentioned in New York.

"It's good to talk with you, Oscar. I don't get many through here that I have much time with. There's something different about you. Something special. You seem so much older than your years."

She told me I was the youngest slave she had ever helped. She asked how I managed to escape and how my parents felt about me setting out on my own. I didn't have the heart to burden her with the truth, but I couldn't lie to her either. "All my mama ever wanted for me was to be free. I'm carrying her to freedom with me, ma'am." We both had teary eyes after that.

On the third morning, Jackson had still not returned, and I feared the worst. When Mrs. Whitfield came to bring me breakfast, I asked, "What if Jackson don't come back today?"

"We wait. It's a long walk by foot. We need to give him another day. Maybe two more. He might have seen soldiers and might be hiding. Just be patient. And trust in Jackson."

She must've known I was getting very restless down in the cellar because of all the rapid-fire questions I threw at her every time she came down to see me. The next time she came, she brought a book. It was a dictionary. "Now, about those words I told you I'd help you with?"

I was excited when my dictionary lesson started with grammar.

"If you know the parts of speech, how to make a sentence, it's easier to understand words." She went on to use a simple sentence. *My name is Oscar.* I liked her example. She then explained a noun, verb, and object.

Heading into dizzying confusion, I shook my head.

"Fine. We'll slow down," she smiled. "Give me a word you know."

"Strawberry," I laughed. Where that came from, I have no idea. But it was funny and laughter felt good. It's strange how ideas pop into your head. Before I knew it, I wrote that word in the dirt. And another and another until we were both laughing.

That night, I heard the familiar pattern of tapping on the back door. It was the doctor. He told the missus that Jackson was due any time. Sure enough, in the middle of the night, he returned and slept beside me, snoring. Relief washed over me like a cool breeze on hot summer afternoon.

The Day I Saw the Hummingbird

Chapter Twenty-Seven

The missus told us that Doctor Edgewood examined Mr. Whitfield. Sure enough, it was a broken bone in his right thigh; it wasn't bad, though. Wrapping it up properly and keeping it still was all he needed. The doctor said he should be up on both feet in several weeks. Until then, he couldn't bear weight on that leg or go up and down stairs. That left Mrs. Whitfield to continue to tend to our needs.

Jackson discovered (and the doctor confirmed) that battles were being fought fairly close to the trail we planned on taking. He told me that while on his way to fetch Doctor Edgewood, he had a close call with danger when he heard horse and foot movements. It was well after sundown. As the cricket sounds filled the darkness, so did marching feet. They must've decided, like we did, that it was better to travel when it was cooler. As Jackson relayed the event, I thought of the time Mama went to the Coleson's house to help the dehydrated soldiers. They were fools to wear heavy wool uniforms during the hot, sun-scorched daytime. I figured that word must've finally gotten out for them to travel after the heat lowered at dusk.

"I shook so hard, I feared they hear my body banging on the ground," said Jackson.

So, we could no longer feel safe traveling at night. I swallowed hard. "Ooh," I moaned. Noticing Jackson's stiffened body, I asked, "When we gonna travel and not get spotted?"

Without waiting for an answer, we said at the same time, "Never."

Hearing our voices in unison made us laugh. It ended when Jackson started choking with giddiness.

Although not outside where we could be easily heard, we had kept our voices at whisper-level down in the cellar. We knew that we could be discovered by a stranger's visit at any time. The sobering realization ended my lightheartedness. Our laughter had gotten pretty loud and, for once, I was the responsible one when I said, "Shh!"

It was no use. Jackson could no more control his laughter than I could control my nervousness. The louder he became, the more sourness rose from my gut. Finally, he caught his breath and he settled down. He wiped his face clear of the tears that escaped with the laughter. "Oh, that feel good," he smiled.

Sitting quietly, I waited for him to collect himself.

Once contained, he said, "From what I seen, soldiers, they move early at night. Later it get quieter and I reckon they was resting. Best traveling time for us is a few hours before daybreak."

"You see any fighting?"

"No, but I done heard shots."

I probed further. "You see any…" I hesitated. I wasn't sure I wanted to ask the question or hear the answer. "See any dead bodies?"

Jackson became very quiet. Letting out a sigh, he said, "Yeah. Sure enough did."

A twisted knot moved into my throat. My voice sounded scrawny and muzzled. "So, it real close, the fighting?" Biting a nail, my arm started to itch. "How we sure we ain't gonna head right into some big battle?"

"We ain't gonna know," he murmured.

We sat in uneasy silence.

I had to say it. "Maybe we oughta stay put. I mean, if the Whitfields let us."

Jackson slowly shook his head in disagreement.

"At least let's ask," I pleaded.

More silence. I never realized just how loud silence could be.

When the missus brought us the next meal, I did like Mama always told me to do and kept quiet. Scared to offend my hosts and my guide, I didn't mention extending our stopover. Turns out, it was a good thing because she mentioned a similar worry. Mrs. Whitfield feared that we'd be venturing out to our deaths if we headed out, knowing soldiers were in our path. She spoke with the doctor and asked him if he could help. He told her he'd do his best to find out locations of the most concentrated fighting, gather what information he could about the safest routes and get back to her with what he discovered.

She also answered a question I had asked about why the doctor wasn't fighting with the South and tending to soldiers. "We're lucky he stayed back to take care of women and children." She wiped a few loose strands of braided hair from the back of her neck. "Not everyone joined up," she said. Curling her upper lip in disgust, she added, "Some with legitimate excuses, like Doctor Edgewood, weren't frowned upon for not fighting. They were the ones who didn't fall under the fervent wrath of the Confederate Army for not helping to defend the South."

When she left us to our meal, I thought about how remarkable it was that so many people involved themselves in helping to free slaves. "That's a heap of trouble for these people," I commented to Jackson. "What happen to white folk caught helping slaves?

"Don't think you wanna hear. None of it good from what I hear tell."

Contemplating the worst, I let it go. "I ain't never thought folk like the Whitfields be willing to risk they own life for folk like us."

He patted my back. "Them people…it what they do, Oscar. Ain't never heard a complaint out of a one of them."

Contemplating what complete strangers risked helping Negroes left me quiet. I couldn't stop thinking about it, pondering what I'd ever be able to do to return the kindness. My attention went to the two books beside me. I patted the Bible Kitch gave me and looked at the dictionary the missus left. All those words, an entire book filled with nothing but words and definitions, and here I was at a complete loss for any words to express myself.

Picking up the dictionary, I recalled Mrs. Whitfield explaining the parts of speech and telling me that every word had its proper place in grammar. Like a doctor learns about bones and muscles, I wanted to learn about that book. I knew it was the way to better myself. I thought of how fortunate it was that Mr. Whitfield's brother and his wife were teachers. I wondered how it would feel to be in school and properly learn. Slaves didn't have that opportunity. I couldn't help feeling foolish that I ignored the missus when she first offered to teach me new words. Thankfully, she came back with the dictionary.

"Jackson," I whispered.

"Yeah?"

"Can you read? And write words?"

"Some," he tilted his head, his big eyes squinting at me.

"How'd you come to learn?"

"A nice man." His voice sounded gravelly. "At one of them safe houses." He reached for a glass of water and took a sip. "During a snow storm. Me and an escapee were getting pretty bored holed up in an attic."

"Attic?"

"Some places got spaces between the roof and the ceiling where runaways can hide. That be an attic. Other places, like here, we hide in cellars. And some places hide us in barn lofts."

"Are them attic ones and lofts ones dangerous? Too easy to find runaways?"

"Yeah, but folks offer what they got. There was this hiding place in an attic I hid in. Had a fake wall we done crawled behind. Covered up with some kind of storage rack on wheels. I heard tell of some pretty creative hiding places."

"Like what?"

"Fake ceiling or wall in a house. Space dug in the ground under animal straw and feed."

As I imagined being in those tight spaces, I wanted to stand and stretch. My calves were cramped from being in one position too long. I straightened my legs and flexed my muscles until the pain subsided. "So, you was in that attic when you learned reading and writing?"

"One day, the man, Mr. Rutherford, come up to the attic with paper and pencil. He write out the alphabet, one letter at a time, and had me say it. Then he put two letters together. Told me they was words and had me say them words out loud. Starting with little words was easy. I remember starting with the word M-E."

"Me," I smiled.

"Then he make it fun. Wrote out other words that rhymed with *me*. *Be* came next. Added another letter and come up with three-letter words rhyming with *me*. *Tea, see,* and *bee*."

"Two different words with same sound, *be* and *bee*? That's funny."

"It get to where it be a lot of fun when he write out words with four letters that still rhyme with *me*."

Having no idea what those words were, I asked, "Like what?"

He didn't respond right away. Instead, he threw it back to me with, "Think of some." His smile was so big, it nearly covered the bottom part of his face.

He was clever getting me to think about what the answer could be. It was another way to learn to use my brain to think through an answer to a question. It took me a few minutes. Just when I became frustrated and was about to give up, out popped, "Free?"

He nodded approval.

"How you spell free?" I asked.

"Has four letters, don't it? Rhymes with *me*," he hinted.

Satisfied that I came up with one of the words he had in mind, I was equally frustrated that I had no idea how to spell it. I struggled for a while and gave up. "You tell me."

"Sound it out. Use your alphabet. Go on now, you can do it."

He was right. And I did. After several failed attempts, I realized it started with the letter F. Going through one letter at a time, I filled in the other three. It gave me a great sense of accomplishment. "Why do learning things feel so good?" It wasn't really a question to him, more just pondering out loud.

Regardless, Jackson responded. "Learning is a door."

"Huh?"

"Someone once tell me it a 'figure of speaking.'"

Getting more confused, I shook my head and rubbed a hand over my cheek.

Jackson, taking notice of my growing confusion, tried to explain what he meant. "Think of something hard to talk 'bout 'cause you can't grab hold of it. Like learning. Now, compare it to something easy you can grab hold of. Like a door. A door leads to places, some good, others not. Right? But the door to learning can only be walked through by understanding the alphabet first, then words. You open a door so you can go someplace. You learn so that mind of yours can open up and take you places you ain't never been. If you can read, books can teach you things. Give you pleasure. Books have stories. They have lessons, too."

"What kind of book has lessons?" I asked.

"One of the plantations I was at, there was a cookbook." He continued to tell me about the directions he saw on how to prepare food and baked goods. "The cook tried to explain how to use it. Never got anywhere. But I seen it. Sure enough, it told how to make things. For supper and such."

I thought of Mama preparing meals. Maybe she hadn't learned from a book how to cook a meal, but she sure did learn from somewhere. I told Jackson, "Ain't just books do that. Spoken learning, too, right?"

"Suppose so."

I nodded. "Mama tell me things to help me so I know how to act good and proper. She learn me how to pick sugarcane. And that I best listen. Keep my mouth shut. My mama taught me a lot about how to get on in the world."

"Guess she could have made her own book," said Jackson.

"She sure could, Jackson. She sure could."

Next time Mrs. Whitfield came down, I relayed the conversation Jackson and I had. And I told her I was ready for more learning. "If you got time," I said politely.

"Of course, I have plenty of time to help you," she smiled.

The Day I Saw the Hummingbird

Chapter Twenty-Eight

While the missus was teaching me to expand my vocabulary and read the dictionary, we also learned we'd be running into the thick of the war if we stayed on the course we had planned. Mississippi, she told us, was the second state to declare its secession from the United States and was steeped in good old southern *fight-till-the-death* pride. The sarcasm in her tone did not go unnoticed.

"Which state done left first?" I asked.

"South Carolina." She proceeded to explain that it was the farthest state to the east, boarding on the Atlantic Ocean. A long way from where we were sitting. Despite what I'd heard from Jackson and what the missus told us, I hoped the fighting was heavier over there near the ocean and was sparse where we'd be traveling.

My hopes were dashed when Mrs. Whitfield cleared her throat and said, "The President of the Confederate States, Mr. Jefferson Davis, is from Mississippi. Word is, a lot of the battles are concentrated in this direction because of him. He has high command and support." She had kept up on the news from the few travelers who came by, family, and newspapers her husband had obtained when he had been out doing business before his accident. "We've got friends who know him. A family that has a plantation near his. Mr. Davis owns over fifty slaves on his large cotton plantation."

Owns slaves ricocheted in my head, like a bullet bouncing off a rock. Those two words reminded me of Prescott. He treated us worse than property, much worse than his dog, Buddy. I shook the sourness of those memories away, like the taste of the few tart berries I had eaten in the forest that had made me sick. Instead, I focused on Jackson and Mrs. Whitfield and the future. The honey-sweet taste of freedom swirled around on my tongue. Once savored, it was an easy notion to swallow.

When the missus' voice came back into focus, she was saying something about the defense of the Mississippi River. I had heard that it was the main artery from north to south. Soldiers would be fiercely protecting it. Kitch probably told me. Maybe Jackson. I had to ask what a "main artery" was. I squinted a confused look and asked.

Mrs. Whitfield apologized for using a word I didn't know and explained it was a central waterway.

Jackson leaned in, like an idea hit him. "If it more heavy along the main waterways, maybe we best head east, then go north." He said that we'd move east across Mississippi to Alabama. From there we could go north, and that would put us in the middle of Tennessee instead of along the Mississippi River.

I liked the sound of that. But I remembered what Kitch said about staying near the water for survival. "What'll we do for water if we stay away from the Mississippi River?"

The tension in my neck muscles relaxed when I saw him smile at my question. "Plenty of waterways in both states. Staying away from large rivers like the Mississippi, where all the fighting is, I reckon we'll be safe enough."

The missus, nodding agreement, said, "Yes. That sounds like a smart plan."

My nervousness eased even more.

Talk of geography, soldiers and battles ended as the missus patted the dictionary. The conversation shifted to my next new lesson. We were at it for a while when she heard my stomach growl. She looked at the watch she wore on a locket around her neck. "My, how the time moves by." Smiling, she closed the cover of the book.

Curiosity had taken me once again. As she was rising to leave the space, I said. "That there timepiece." I motioned to it with my forehead. "How'd you learn to read it?"

Her eyes lit up. "My papa taught me to tell time. He taught me many things." Then her eyes dulled, and nostalgia came through with her words. "I remember my excitement when I learned to tell time. I ran to my nanny shouting, 'Guess what I can do?' And oh, how I bubbled with pride. Mildred always encouraged me to question things. To learn about everything I could set my eyes and ears on. Working with you, Oscar, reminds me of those sweet times."

Poor Mrs. Whitfield. It didn't take much to hoist up her pain from events that happened years ago. That got me worrying for two reasons: I had to be careful not to cause her unnecessary grief because of my questions, and it got me wondering if the burning ache from losing Mama and Sammy would ever go away. Not knowing what else to do, I tightened my lips into a forced smile and said nothing further.

Mrs. Whitfield, being the sweet, sensitive person she was, said, "I'll teach you to tell time." She reached to touch her watch. For a brief moment, she was lost in thought before she refocused her delicate eyes on mine. There was no end to the generosity of that gracious woman.

When she left to fix our meal, Jackson put a hand on my shoulder. "It be a good thing, that appetite for learning of yours. Mighty fine quality, Oscar. Grab hold of every chance you can to better yourself. Yessiree! I done proud to know folk like you."

"Thanks. But I don't wanna upset or bother kindly folk," I responded.

"Never you mind 'bout bothering nobody. The missus, she offered her help. Doing you both a powerful lot of good. You see how she turned all bright-eyed when you asked 'bout her timepiece?" He shook his smiling head. "I tell you what Oscar, you just keep at being yourself. Fill yourself up with as much knowledge as folk are willing to share."

Bright eyes, yeah. But then she looked so sad. She seems so different than that first night when we arrived. I couldn't help wondering if there was something upsetting her, under the surface of her original cheerful demeanor.

Eventually, I would come to understand the deep sorrow she harbored; but it wouldn't be from her or during this stopover.

Responding to my silence, Jackson asked, "You good?"

Snapping out of my reflection of the missus, I said to him, "Just thinking."

"That'll get you in trouble," he grinned.

When I looked at him and thought of all the attention Mrs. Whitfield gave to me, I could swear that the little candlelight in the space grew in intensity. *It sure don't take much to fill a soul with warmhearted feelings.* "Jackson."

"Yes, Oscar."

"You a good friend."

***

Doctor Edgewood returned to check on Mr. Whitfield. He confirmed that the heaviest fighting was along the Mississippi River. None of us were surprised.

Our last day at the Whitfield's home was spent discussing when we'd leave, what supplies and food the missus would send with us, and where our next safe house would be. There was a safe house halfway up the center of Alabama, situated in a deep forest area like where we were. By foot, we could get there in a little over a week…if everything went smoothly.

Our last meal was one of the best I ever tasted: flavored black-eyed peas, fried okra, savory rice, and sweet honey on cornbread. The missus made plenty with the intent of sending food along with us in the form of ready-to-eat cakes. As the light from the cracks in the wooden wall dulled, we knew it was getting late. It was time for the plans and conversations to end.

With my belly and heart full, we settled in for sleep. No sooner did I nod off than I jolted awake in a cold sweat from a bad dream. Jackson, happily snoring, remained undisturbed. I shook my drenched head to rid it of the sickening images of Negro men hanging from trees, their faces a blur. A distant, imagined thumping sound of a body being dragged from a horse sent spasms to my muscles. Those thudding hooves on boggy ground haunted me.

Trying everything I could think of to quiet the craziness going on between my ears was of no use. The rest of the night wore on. Jackson slept, and I fidgeted. When it was close to the time to leave, I was wound up as tight as a banjo string. We were leaving the Whitfield's safety and hospitality and walking right into the white man's battle. On purpose! Jackson said we couldn't stay where we were and I didn't want to leave. I was downright scared. Back at the Coleson's plantation, working to the bone under those cruel conditions, I never felt trapped. But I felt trapped down in that cellar, listening to Jackson snore and fearing what was outside awaiting us. I used to be able to shift my attention off my worry to something else like a tree, a bird, or even a candle. I reached for the unlit candle and felt its melted top and streams of solidified wax down the sides. I imagined seeing it, but all I could see were flames engulfing Mama, Pursey, Sammy, all my people. I grabbed hold of my scalp and squeezed it. *Stop! Leave me alone!*

I forced myself to envision something pleasant. A magnolia tree. I visualized the leathery evergreen leaves and buds slowly opening into fragrant white flowers. Oh, how I loved to see the new blooms in spring and smell the scents. Just as I was starting to calm, a hummingbird flew into my made-up picture. This hummingbird was a sparkling bluish-green. I'd never seen that color before or since. Its wings were flapping as fast as my heartbeat. My chest pounded as that beautiful feathered creature brought back the day I last saw a hummingbird. Grief swelled up and overcame me.

Jackson woke up. He looked over at me and saw me dripping in perspiration with tears streaming down my cheeks. He shot up from his bed. "What happened?"

"Bad dreams. Bad memories." My arms trembled.

"Wanna talk?"

"No!" I bit a nail.

"Whatcha need, Oscar?"

Spitting out the nail that I had just chewed off, I moaned, "We gonna be killed." I looked up at the ceiling to the door—the door to our supposed freedom. "We walk out that door and we gonna be surrounded!"

"Oscar, calm down. You was fine yesterday."

"Says who?" I pouted.

"Wasn't you enjoying the learning?" Jackson moved closer to me, the heat of his body warm on my side. "And the meal? Now, that was some fine cooking! A pure act of love from the missus."

The missus. Just the mention of her name allowed me to breathe easier. It enabled me to speak my mind. "Jackson." I hesitated.

"I'm here, Oscar." His voice sounded soft, relaxed. "I'm here."

I listened to his breathing, slow and even through his nose. I felt soothed by his presence. "I'm scared..."

"I know. Me, too."

"You ain't sounding scared," I said.

"Learned to control it, Oscar. Don't mean I ain't feeling it."

"How?" I turned to face him. "How you hide it?"

My friend put a hand on my back and told me to take a deep, slow breath.

I did.

He then asked me to think of one thing, only one, that made me feel good.

"Like what?"

"Anything. How 'bout a piece of that there cornbread the missus done made for us?" Jackson's eyes had a twinkle to them.

Magically, I smiled.

Seeing my change in mood, he said. "Good. Now just keep thinking of that there cornbread all honeyed-up."

I did. The quivering in my arms settled down.

"Real good, Oscar. Good job. When you get them bad ideas, just switch your thinking to good ones. Pick one good thing and keep on thinking that one good thought till you ain't so scared. That's what I do. Learned that when I were young." Scratching the back of his head, his attention went inside himself, like he was remembering something. "Long time ago…Well, now, here we are and I'm passing it along to you."

I nodded. Taking in a deep, even breath, I said, "Jackson, thank you."

It wouldn't be until I got older that I learned the word "sincerely," but what I meant to say to Jackson was, "I *sincerely* thank you, 'cause you keep saving my life."

The Day I Saw the Hummingbird

Chapter Twenty-Nine

My heart felt like it had been squeezed into my throat as Jackson and I stood at the door with the Whitfields. The missus was in a fine lavender dress with a beige lace collar, atop it hung her locket watch. On her cheeks was a pinch of rose rouge. Her eyes were misty, like mine. The mister, with the aid of crutches and his right leg bent, was at her side. She handed a thin cloth bag to Jackson. "There should be enough food for a few days."

"Thank you, ma'am. Mighty kind of you for all you done for us."

She reached a hand to his shoulder. "It's been good for us to have you here. And thank *you* for helping me with Maxwell." She was referring to her husband and the journey Jackson took to fetch the doctor. She then turned to me with the dictionary in her hand. "I want you to have this."

I put my hand on the edge where the cover met the pages. "Oh, no. I ain't taking your dictionary. That's yours, ma'am."

"I've another," she said. "This one is yours."

When I held out my palms to receive it, her warm goodbye touch saddened me. I held the dictionary upright and out slipped an envelope with my name on it. It fell to the floor. I bent to pick it up, looked up to her and asked, "For me?"

"Yes, Oscar. Inside is another letter addressed to Mr. and Mrs. Terrance Whitfield, our family in New York City." Reaching for my hands clutching the dictionary and envelope, she continued. "I'm hoping you will see your way to their home. Once you do, this is a letter of introduction to our family." She looked at her husband and let loose a stream of tears. Returning her gaze my way, she said, "We both feel that they can help you. Not just with work, but continuing on with your education."

I just about fell to the floor overwhelmed by what this most wonderful couple had offered me. They gave me the promise of something more than freedom—I now had the possibility of a future with meaning. I didn't even know such a thing was possible. "I, I…" Words got stuck in my mouth.

Jackson patted my side. "You done created a miracle, Missus Whitfield. I do believe Oscar done lost his tongue."

We all laughed. The momentary cheer ended when Mrs. Whitfield gave me a hug. And did the same to Jackson. That was the first time a white person hugged me. I will never forget it—the warmth of her body, the compassionate closeness, and the sense of belonging that transcended skin color. The missus and I wiped our tears as we finished our goodbyes with handshakes with Mr. Whitfield.

I turned to face the open door. The view outside that door looked calm enough on the surface, but awfully dangerous because of all the threats my mind saw. Once again, there we were, a conductor and a fugitive slave, both traveling without authorization or papers. We entered the dark night praying we'd make it to the next safe house. Or even the next night.

We headed east into the dense Mississippi forest that first night. I'm not sure how far we walked, but it was a long distance. We started out determined to keep up a good pace and put as many miles behind us as we could, but by the second night, we were too exhausted to continue on like that. Near dawn, we found a group of tall trees to rest by. It was then we heard the sound of distant horses approaching.

"Get down!" Jackson whispered.

We dove behind a high knoll of soil and dead bush. Jackson covered me in leaves and did the same to himself.

I held my breath and waited.

The noises of horses and riders grew louder. Snapping branches. Swishing brush. Snorts. Leather creaking. Men grunting. Hooves clip-clopping.

Those sounds sent shivers up and down my body, but I was glad for them because they drowned out the drumbeat of my heart, which sounded like thunder to me.

It sounded like a formation of soldiers rode by only several feet from where we were hiding. They sent a cloud of dust I could see from the tiny air hole Jackson had left me while covering my body. If any of those soldiers had bothered to look our way, all they'd have seen was lumps of leaves. Good old Jackson.

The next sound I heard was the slurping of water. Lots of slurping.

Then leather creaking, some voices I had to say sounded normal, and pounding horse hooves.

Then silence.

We waited a long time before moving. Finally, Jackson said, "They just stop for watering the horses. Themselves, too, most probably."

I hadn't realized that we were so close to a pool in a shallow creek, a watering hole. "You see anything? Was they soldiers? How many?" My blood still racing, I talked so fast my speech was a blur. "I didn't see nothing."

"Me neither. But," he coughed, "sounded like two, maybe three horses. Probably a posse." He laughed.

"Why you laughing?"

"Nerves." He snorted to clear his nose. "But, maybe not a posse. Could be they was friendly. We ain't the only ones traveling these here woods."

Not wanting to feel so fearful and alone, I wanted to believe it was possible that there were others like us close by. After all, that's how I met Jackson.

While we stayed put, I looked at the small hill that hid us and thought of the mound of dirt covering Mama's grave. I wondered if, in our travels, I had walked on any unmarked graves with no evidence remaining on the landscape, like my mama's. Marked or not, those were sacred places—burial grounds of loved ones left behind out of necessity, not choice. I thought of something Macy had told us after Pursey was buried. There was talk about there not being a Negro cemetery for our people to rest in. Mrs. Coleson was upset about how Pursey died and asked her husband, "Why can't you dedicate a plot of land somewhere for a burial site?" Word was she thought it wrong to not respect the dead, no matter their skin color.

The master disagreed. Macy said he said something like, "They're my property. I'll bury them where I want."

"Not even a casket?" asked the missus. Macy said Mrs. Coleson was sniffing here, probably crying. She didn't catch the rest of the conversation that left her feeling cold, like the corpses in the ground.

A hot flush moved through me, and a deep feeling of anger rose in my belly. It grew in strength like a dark, cloudy storm building in the summer sky. Stronger and stronger it came. Then it burst! I threw the leaves off my body and stood. Stomping a foot, I startled Jackson.

"What?" he quickly got up. Instinctively grabbing hold of me, "Get back down!" he whispered.

"No!" I'd had it. My pain had resurfaced and wanted to have its way. Once again, I was victim to my impulse for revenge. I wanted something—someone—to make the madness stop inside of me. I want it to stop for all the Negroes subjugated to indignities and torture day after day who must be feeling the same as me. Kicking leaves and scattering them into a swirling cloud of hostility, I jerked away from Jackson.

Jackson pounced on me and brought me to the ground. Into my ear, once again, he said, "Settle down! If you can't do it for you, then do it for me."

I heard him.

"I got work to do," he said. "You wanna make them nasty folk pay? Then lemme do my work freeing you. And others after you. How you think that'll make them bad slave owners feel?"

Again, I heard him. And with his words, took a breath, and calmed. A little.

He shouted another whisper right into my ear. "You go sticking your neck out, they gonna kill you! Then you just one more dead nigger." His voice cracked when he said, "They ain't gonna care. You let them get to you, then your life ain't been for nothing. Make that life you got mean something."

Another slow deep breath and I felt even calmer.

He relaxed his grip on my arm. "Good. You smart, Oscar. Get another lung-full of air."

I did.

Jackson pulled me close. Holding me, he said. "You just a boy. You seen too much for a young age." His voice turned soft and weepy. "I know. I know…"

Feeling his warm arms around me, the comfort of a friend, I broke down. The anger melted into a stream of tears. It felt like my insides were having a bath as I continued to cry my heart out.

Jackson kept quiet for the longest time then said, "Let's get us some rest." But before he completely let me go, continued. "You remember next time you get that killing urge, you keep your head. Promise me that."

I wanted to promise that to him, but I knew a promise meant I'd have to keep my word. Mama would never let me forget that when she'd tell me more than once, *sometime your word be all you got. Don't never lie. And when you give a vow to someone, you best be keeping it.* Promising Jackson meant honoring Mama. I didn't know that I could.

When I didn't respond, Jackson did. "I need me a promise!"

The force in his voice, commanding me, sounded like Mama. Again, the tears came and I knew I had to consent. I nodded my head but kept my lips tight.

The Day I Saw the Hummingbird

Seeing the nod that indicated agreement to his wish, he said, "I trust in you, Oscar. Don't you be letting me down. Now, let's get us some rest."

I moved my hand over the dry, powdery soil, moving pebbles, twigs and whatever else was left there by the wind until my mind went still. By the time I finally came to my senses, the sun had hit a high, bright place in the sky. The temperature must have climbed over thirty degrees to what felt like a sweltering, humid ninety-degrees. I had two layers of clothes on, making my bag lighter to carry. When I could no longer tolerate the heat, I removed my outer shirt and tucked it in with the rest of my things. Wet clothes stuck to my skin as my body continued to drip sweat. Jackson had fallen asleep, so I let him be. I finished the small amount of water we had. Before long, my mouth became dry, and it felt like a boulder was bouncing around in my head. I became nauseated. Torn between wanting to get up to get more water at the nearby creek and fear of being seen, I remained where I was.

By the time Jackson moaned and stirred awake, I was dry heaving and weak.

"Lordy, what done happened to you?"

The Day I Saw the Hummingbird

I couldn't answer because my legs cramped up, causing me to hunch over in agony. I was real dizzy, too.

He put one hand to my skin and went into action.

I don't remember him dragging my body to water. All I recall is waking up still fully clothed, soaked from head-to-toe, on the side of the creek.

"Welcome back! You give 'ole Jackson quite a scare." Jackson's eyes were wide, and it seemed as if every muscle in his face was coiled up too tight.

I was still on the ground, trying to gather my wits. Back on the plantation, I had seen many a slave fall victim to the sun's boiling rays. Especially since Prescott wouldn't give us water. That's what must have happened to me. I still felt shaky when I said, "Don't worry. I'm fine."

"No, you ain't." He put a cold hand on my arm. "Not as yet. You still hot as the Devil's armpit. We still gotta cool you off some." He had me sip some water. "Take it slow or you gonna get sick again."

He kept giving me sips of cool, fresh water until the banging in my head calmed, and my tongue stopped sticking to the roof of my mouth. I was glad my stomach stopped heaving. After I don't know how long, when I felt a return of energy, I told him, "I feel better. Honest. I do."

Nodding like he believed me, "Good. We gonna wait a scrap longer to be sure." After a long while, he was satisfied I was back to normal. It was nightfall, and he said, "Let's get a move on. But we gonna take it easy." He filled our water containers, and we grabbed our things.

If we thought our big problems were over for a while, we were sorely mistaken. Mosquitoes descended upon us as we made our way through the thickly wooded area. They ferociously attacked. I was covered in bites; Jackson was, too. But I scratched my skin raw while Jackson had the sense to leave his skin alone.

Into the night we moved, my arms itching like crazy. I swatted my skin hoping the sting from the slap would calm the itch. Nothing I did—no physical or mental tricks—stopped me from itching. Everything made it worse. Every bush, every prickly leaf, or tall grass that rubbed against me started a crawling sensation screaming from one part of my crusted-over body to every other part. Miserably, I trudged on until we both collapsed from fatigue.

Down next to a marshy area, Jackson grabbed a handful of mud and covered his exposed, bug-bitten skin. "Stops the air from hitting them bites. Calms the itching."

Copying him, I covered myself in mud. The relief was instant. "You sure do know an awful lot about an awful lot, Jackson."

"Ah. Just pick handy things up here and there." He gave me a tired smile.

I gave him one back. As I set my bag down, I felt the two books I was carrying: the Bible and the dictionary. I wanted to learn everything—every word and idea those books could teach me and all the wisdom it takes to be a good man like Jackson.

I welcomed the undisturbed sleep of an unshackled soul.

Chapter Thirty

After traveling another two days, my skin was raw, my feet hurt, and my head felt like a drum was beating inside it. With a throbbing headache and gurgling belly, I was too hungry to think of much other than eating. Hours ago, we had consumed the last of Mrs. Whitfield's food. Jackson had been so helpful and tolerant that I didn't want to whine, complain, or beg him to stop for a rest. So, I nearly fell to my knees to kiss the ground when he spotted a large stream and asked, "Wanna take a break and catch us some fish?"

We hid our things, looked for gators, and listened for any dangerous sounds. Nothing other than the familiar voices of the forest sang out to us. He stripped down to his underwear and plunged headfirst into the cool water. Refreshing spray hit my face. He dove where the bottom wasn't visible, but I didn't have his confidence. I found a place to enter where I could see rocks on the bottom. The colors of big rocks caught my attention: brown, tan, black, red, and ones jutting out of the water covered in slimy grassy moss. I wondered why they all looked different. Looking around at the thick foliage, I noticed various shades of green. I never realized how many different kinds of green colors made up a forest. I guess there was more to green than I thought.

I came to the conclusion that there was more to just about everything I had, up to that moment, taken for granted. And that got me thinking. How did everything come to be? I looked up through the tangled branches of a tree shading the water to a few big, white, fluffy clouds drifting overhead. And I thought of Mama. *Look to all this beauty God give us.* She'd touch a flower and say, *that flower be a miracle.* She used to say that nature and all that was put before us to see were miracles. *God's work.* Maybe it was her love of nature that brought her to God. In all my young years, I'd never entertained that before. But why would I, just a kid, think about such things? All of a sudden, I noticed! Everything that was around me—what my eyes beheld, my ears heard, my nose smelled, my skin felt, and even what my mind could conjure—was a wonderful mystery. Maybe I could solve this grand mystery with enough curiosity and studying. And help from people like Jackson and Mrs. Whitfield.

Nature's magical glory lifted my spirits as high as the moon.

My breathing came easy as the calm, slow-moving, shallow current flowed along the banks. It allowed me to see fish floating just under the surface.

"Look here." Jackson pointed to a solitary fish that appeared to be around two pounds. It was circling a group of smaller silvery swimming prey. The smaller ones, no longer than a half-inch, caught in the larger fish's movement spread their fins and scattered. The largemouth predator sprang up and grabbed several in his mouth then plunged back under a pile of rocks to feast.

Jackson put a finger to his lips, indicating to keep quiet, then dove under. When he surfaced, he had the big wiggling fish in his left hand. He splashed out of the water, held the flopping thing until it stopped moving, and then started a little fire.

Still dripping, I stood beside him. "How'd you do that?" All I knew from what Kitch taught me was how to fish with a spear. Jackson used his bare hands.

"Grip the lower jaw with your thumb and first finger." He made a grasping motion, like a clamp to show me. "They pretty fast and can slip away, but you hold tight. That 'ole fish ain't eating his supper, he our supper!"

"Don't it bite?"

"Oh sure, them teeth leave a nasty mark, but you gotta catch a bunch before it shows real bad."

Saliva dripped from the sides of my lips as I watched him cook our meal. When he held out my half, Jackson laughed. My stomach growled so loudly, it nearly made an echo. Next to Mama's cooking and that last supper from Mrs. Whitfield, this was some of the tastiest food I ever had. Maybe not itching to death had something to do with how much I enjoyed that meal, too. My skin felt better after having been dipped in the coolness of the water minutes before. Filled with fish and thankfulness, I watched Jackson devour his portion.

After the hours of walking, the refreshing stream and a good meal, I was tired to the bone. Night had fallen. I knew we should get up and keep going, but I didn't want to. "We gonna head out?"

Jackson smiled at me. "You looking tired. Let's have us a rest for a couple hours. Then we'll get a move on."

I could've hugged him right then and there. Instead, I reclined under the cover of twisted branches. Watching the movement of the sky—twinkling stars and gently shifting fluffs of grayish-white covering the brightness of the night's light—I turned on my side to look at Jackson. He wasn't yet asleep. "Jackson," I mumbled.

"Yeah?"

"You ever think about God?"

"Hmm," he sighed. "Not sure I much do."

"Me neither. But today, I had a feeling. I dunno. I just got to thinking. Well, not much. Thinking I mean."

"Yeah, that'd be a good thing," he gently chuckled.

"It felt new...like coming from a place different than inside my head."

"Hmm, sound like that active stuff 'tween your ears is quieting down. That be good."

Deep in my own contemplation, overcome with unexplainable emotions, I hardly heard what he just said. "My mama, she seemed to feel Him. The Lord. Never was real to me till today." I hesitated, then continued, "Jackson..."

"Yeah, Oscar, I'm still here," he laughed.

"Where'd all this come from? Like the color of them silvery fish, and the color of...of everything. And everything else? Ever wonder 'bout them things."

"Oscar, for a young'un, you sure sounding like a grown-up, what with all them questions. Best I can say is I dunno."

"My mama used to tell me I grown up fast. Said I had wisdom, whatever that means."

"Your mama, she sound like she did good by you."

"She sure did. You'd of liked her. Everybody did. 'Cept mean Prescott." I explained what happened to Mama her last day on this earth. A heaviness moved into my body as I told the story and I cried. This time the crying stung less. When I was done and the memory started to fade, I felt a little lighter. My attention went to a breeze gently sighing through a tree. When the air stilled and the rustling leaves stopped moving, I felt as if nature had just mirrored my mood. Feelings surface and move on mysteriously. I thought of Jackson explaining the door example in the Whitfield's cellar that had confused me earlier. I finally understood how connecting unrelated things can shed light on whatever might be puzzling me. The movement in life or in nature was no different than the movement in my head. Those leaves were like my thoughts; they rustled around for a while, and then they settled down for a while.

"Jackson," I muttered, wanting to share my discovery.

"Uh-huh." His voice trailed, sleep had started to grab him.

I left his name hanging in the air he snored in. And just before I joined him, I looked at my bag, containing the Bible and dictionary. I wondered if, someday, those books would help me understand some of the mystifying questions I had.

* * *

Having slept for a good while, I felt refreshed as we headed out in the dark of night. A breeze picked up and rustled plants as we made our way. After several uneventful hours, we saw what looked like a body lying on the ground. Jackson stopped me with the back of his arm. I moved to hide behind a large, wide tree while he went to see what was there.

He came back clearly shaken. His bowed head and downcast eyes gave me a really bad feeling. Grabbing hold of my shoulder, he turned me around and said, "We heading in another direction."

"Why?" My voice cracked.

Without answering, he continued to push my back to move me away from what he had just seen.

Insistent, I stopped to face him. "Tell me. My nerves gonna be bad if I get to wondering why we ain't..." I paused when I saw the fear in his wide-open eyes, eyebrows slanted upward. "What you see?"

"Oh," he moaned. Rubbing his forehead, he said, "Last thing you need is more bad pictures in that young head."

Jackson always wanted to protect me from the rotten parts of reality. Didn't he know by now that I wanted to hear whatever the truth was? I persisted, "Best tell me. You know how my head runs wild. Ain't no truth worse than what my mind can conjure."

"That there's a fair point, Oscar." He heaved a big sigh. "She were a slave. They beat her pretty bad and left her...um...naked."

My knees grew weak. "Soldiers or posse that done it?"

"No way of telling who done this."

I felt very insecure. There was probably no place in the South, where the Civil War was being fought, that was safe for an escaped Negro. My voice sounded like a little boy's when I asked Jackson, "What we gonna do now?"

Confirming what I was just feeling, he said, "We keep going on in the direction we was headed and be extra careful. Keep extra quiet, too." When I silently nodded my agreement, he started to move toward where the dead body was. "Don't be looking. Just keep your eyes fixed straight ahead."

He tried to cover my view by walking close in front of me, but I broke loose and saw her. In hindsight, I'm sorry I did. That particular image burned into my brain like so many others. She was stripped of every piece of clothing. Her legs were open and bent at unnatural angles. Her exposed private parts were raw and bloody. Her torso was bruised and cut, and her face was swollen from lips to forehead. I flinched at her shocked, empty eyes and wondered what was the last thing she saw before she met her Maker. What was she thinking?

I may have been young, but I knew about rape. I knew from the horrible nights when Prescott stormed into the women's cabin in a drunken rage. And from when Prescott came for Mama. I knew from conversations with Sammy, who was old enough to know these things. And from hints and whispers from Mama in conversations with Albert and Kitch. No need spell it out, I could easily figure out what happened. A child knows. There it was again, unglued from its submerged place: rage. "Why? Why?"

Jackson quickly covered my mouth with his hand. "Shh."

I rapidly gasped into his palm and let his resistance take hold. Were it not for him holding me, and all he'd done to help, I don't know what I would have done.

"You gonna be quiet if I let go your mouth?"

I couldn't answer. The vision of savage white men violating this poor young woman and leaving her to rot was too much to bear. I wanted to scream and then I remembered Mama's words, *Keep quiet. You gotta know when to shut you mouth.* She said it over and over, especially when I was preparing to escape. *While you on the run, keep still. Get to that freedom.* Rage gave way to disgust. And disgust gave way to sorrow for this poor woman who had been violated and tortured to death. Finally, I nodded. When he removed his hand from my mouth, I kept quiet.

How could there be so much beauty in this world and also so much ugliness? If God created the wonders of nature I had marveled in a few hours ago, did He create this wickedness, too? Could the same God give us people like Mrs. Whitfield and people like Prescott?

The Day I Saw the Hummingbird

Whatever certainty I thought I had while resting at the stream vanished. The future and my place in it felt as clear as the dead of night.

The Day I Saw the Hummingbird

Chapter Thirty-One

I felt like a two-hundred-pound sack of sugar was weighing down on my body. The longer we walked, the more hopeless I became. Who was she, the unjustly disgraced young woman? And who were the evil men who did that to her? I was young but not too young to question hatred. To feel its effect in my bones, muscles, lungs, every inch of my living flesh. It sickened me. There was nothing that was going to erase her from my mind. Her contorted, tortured face and twisted body covered in blood and left in the dirt haunted me. What did her tormenters feel? I know how their actions made me feel: disheartened and furious. Their senseless act of violence stole my appetite and robbed me of sleep. How could some people be so vicious?

It angered me that I was victim to what I'd seen, not just with that unfortunate woman but also with all the needless suffering I'd encountered. Feeling like I was breathing through molasses, my chest felt compressed, and I struggled to take in a lung-full of air. The longer we walked, the harder it was to get my thoughts off the brutal culprits. I'd like to have seen their faces and wrapped my hands around their necks. It made me feel bad to picture killing someone, but I could no more help the hell I sank to than I could bring any of those poor souls back to life. That familiar trapped feeling grabbed hold and wouldn't let go. No matter how far behind Louisiana was on the map, the plantation weighed on me like the bag I carried on my back. Prescott's evil had scorched and singed deep wounds into every inch of my mind that felt like they'd never heal. What he did to me and to the people I loved replayed in my memory every time I came across something horrible along the way to freedom.

My misery was interrupted when Jackson lost his footing on a loose rock.

"Oh!" He fell to the ground. He grabbed hold of his left ankle.

Seeing the pain digging into his usually easy expression, I snapped out of my mood.

"You hurt bad?" I knelt down beside him.

Feeling his foot and leg for injury, he said, "Don't reckon so. Lemme stand and see." When I reached over to offer to help him, he said, "Lemme try and get up on my own." He bent his hurt limb on top his good one, pressed his hands firm on the ground, then pushed off the leg that wasn't in pain to stand.

Jackson reminded me of Mr. Whitfield on those crutches with his leg flexed to avoid weight. I held my breath as he put his left foot down and shifted his weight. I didn't like the look of his knee shaking and buckling. Then, just as fast as my nervous stomach squeezed something sour into my mouth, he took a hobbling step. "I'm good." His smile was almost as wobbly as his knee.

After a couple more swaying movements, I knew he wasn't going anywhere soon. "Maybe you best get off that leg for a bit?" We'd been at it for quite a long haul and we were both very tired. Plus, I was drained from being scared and upset after seeing that poor dead woman. "Some rest would do us both a world a good."

Jackson looked at me for a long second as if he was trying to make up his mind about something. He finally nodded and smiled. When he spoke, I knew why he was hesitating. "You mighty young for a conductor, Oscar."

I took a step back. "What you talking 'bout?"

"Just saying you made a right good decision just now. If need be, I trust you to see me to the next safe—"

"Whoa! Don't you be talking like that! You know everything and I dunno nothing compared to you."

"One thing for sure. You could do with more learning 'bout how to keep a quieted down voice. Calm one, too." He winked and gave me one of his crooked grins.

I noticed my voice had gotten squeaky. Kicking the ground, I replied in a nice low tone, "Well, least I got me two strong legs. You interested in leaning on them to get over thataway so we can hide?" I pointed to a possible place past some tall shrubs.

We hid in a dried-out gully down a slight slope. Jackson took his shoes off. It didn't take long for the injured ankle to swell to the size of a cantaloupe. I felt squeamish watching his skin color fade to gray.

Worried by what it looked like, I asked, "What you need?" Nodding my forehead toward his foot, "That ain't looking good."

He wiped beads of sweat from his upper lip. "Nothing," he moaned.

"Any fool can see you gonna need help. Tell me, what you want me to do?"

He looked around and pointed to a limb of a tree that was a few feet away. "That there," he motioned with a finger. "Cut off that lower part and bring it here."

I grabbed the knife and did what he said. He then instructed me on how to shave the top flat. "That there'll be my cane."

"No! Ain't no way you gonna make any distance being lame like that."

Craning his neck to face me, he shifted his position. "Lemme rest some first. You ain't seen how quick ole Jackson can mend."

Thankfully, our last meal was a couple hours before and we had enough water to last several hours. Jackson closed his eyes and napped. I joined and awoke before him, feeling much better than I had earlier in the day. I was relieved that my mood shifted and moved on like migrating birds.

Jackson's hoarse snoring subsided, and he suddenly opened his eyes. Looking startled, he said, "I must've been dreaming. One of them times it's good to wake up."

"A bad one?"

"Um-hum," he nodded. "Glad I ain't in that dream no more."

I wondered about what he'd dreamed. Was it what he'd experienced conducting slaves from south to north. "Jackson?"

"Yeah," he replied.

"Can I ask you something?"

"Sure, go ahead." He smiled. "Don't mean I'll answer."

I knew he was joking from the lightness in his voice. "Tell me 'bout where you been. What you seen? How many you helped? Are all the white folk along the way as nice as the Whitfields? Do you—"

"Hold on there. You moving faster than a galloping horse. Now, what that first thing?"

I couldn't remember. "I forget," I laughed.

"Well, lemme see. Hmm." He swiped a fly away from his moist foot. Distracted, he commented, "Sure is humid. Days like this my clothes don't dry much from the outside air."

I waited while he picked up a large piece of bark and fanned himself with it. "So," he continued pondering. "Where I been? Well, I been way up to the north of Maryland." The black center of his eyes grew bigger, and he stopped looking at me. Darkness, like a rain cloud drifting in, moved over his face. "Done a lot of walking that time. Started out with two slaves from the bottom of Georgia, near Florida."

"Started out with two?" Confused, I bent my head.

"Yeah, only one made it." He became quiet.

Ignoring his closed, tight lips and painful squinting, I should've let him be. But, no, I asked, "What happened?" Took me a while more of growing up to realize I had to allow someone their emotions in private if they don't appear like they want to talk. Back then, my inquisitiveness took over.

"Was a married couple. She was carrying a baby inside her. Not too far along, I don't reckon." Smacking his lips, he moved the bark to fan the back of his neck. "She done got the vomiting sickness. Couldn't keep liquid in her. They," he sighed, and continued, "paid no heed when I said go back to the plantation, you know, to get her some help. She could've made it back."

"Must've been a bad place they come from."

"Oh, Oscar. One of the worst I seen. Mean foreman like what you told me 'bout Prescott. For no reason, he done terrible things. Don't even wanna repeat them. But lemme tell you, I understand how you feeling 'bout things you seen."

I swallowed hard and waited. Jackson went on to describe that the woman didn't make it. The husband insisted that they bury her with his unborn baby inside her belly. "He stubborn. Wouldn't continue on with me till we done that. That there man was stuck in sorrow rest of the trip."

When he finished telling me about them, his smile had vanished. I felt bad that I had started this conversation and stirred up sadness in him. I thought so hard on how to change the subject that I give myself a headache. "Maryland far?"

"Was for my feet," he half-smiled.

Although brief, it was good to see him try to grin, reminding me of toothless Kitch's similar attempts to make me feel better.

Jackson continued on with shifting the conversation away from sorrowful stories, for both our benefits. "Some make it far up as Canada." When I cocked my head to the side, he explained where Canada was. And he gave me a brief lesson in the geography of the northern free states. I knew a little from map drawings and brief discussions, but after what he said, I had a bigger picture to help me understand.

We chatted some more, mainly with my questions about places, buildings, food, and such, always careful to avoid sad topics. Jackson did most of the talking until his eyes became heavy and he fell back asleep. It was comforting to settle down to the sound of his heavy breathing. I was glad for his company. I didn't ever want to be without it.

The Day I Saw the Hummingbird

Chapter Thirty-Two

I must have dozed off because the next thing I remembered was Jackson gently nudging my shoulder. "Best get a move on."

Still groggy, I rubbed crust off my eyelids, stretched my legs to work out the kinks, and raised myself on an elbow to face him. The changed appearance of his swollen, red, injured ankle startled me. There was no way he'd be able to put his shoe back on with the size of that thing just about double of normal.

"How you gonna walk?" It wasn't really a question. I wanted to convince him that we needed to let it rest and heal. My own banged up hands and feet from working the fields had shown me how long it can take for swelling to go down. He didn't even have anything cool to put on it, like Mama used to do for me.

Jackson rubbed his ankle. His face twisted in the way every person I ever saw who had gotten whipped or beat did. That was all I needed to see. We were headed for big trouble if he walked any distance. "It hurts?" I didn't know what else to say.

"Hell, yeah!" He glared at me.

I jumped from the force in his tone.

When he saw my reaction, his face flushed with shame. He put a hand to his cheek and thought for a minute. "Best not staying in one place too long." His voice softened and the creases on his brow eased.

So did my riled gut. It was his way of apologizing for snapping at me. A mood can change with pain.

"Hanging round here longer put us in a heap more danger of getting caught," he said, looking at our belongings. "If you carry them bags, I can balance on that there cane you made for me, and—"

"But," I interrupted, "how you gonna get that shoe on? You ain't walking barefoot."

Hesitating, his attention went to his bag of clothing. "I got me an idea." He had me take a heavy cotton shirt out of his bag and rip it into large pieces. He then put on a sock and had me tie the strips of material around his foot and ankle. "That gonna fix me up good and proper." When he put his foot down, he winced.

He was clearly in pain, but I knew that suggesting staying put would only annoy him. I just hoped he'd be able to walk well enough to make it to our next destination, which he told me was around six hours away. I grabbed hold of our things and stayed close behind as he slowly hobbled. In what felt like an hour, his speed lessened while his limp got worse. As his movement continued to slow, he looked like a lame animal. Finally, he stopped. "Hold up." His bandage was now covered in blood.

A rush of dizzying panic hit me between the eyes. "You best get off that foot."

This time he didn't protest or insist we keep going. He just nodded pitiful agreement. "There," he pointed to a group of trees surrounded by tall grass and brush, "How 'bout settling there for a bit?" He staggered over to the destination, sat down, and unwrapped the dressing.

I never saw anything turn so bad so fast in all my life. "That don't look good."

His toes were swollen nubs barely distinguishable one from the other, all bloated and covered in blood and green-yellow pus. Threads of wool from his sock were stuck to an open area on top of his foot where a blister had opened and festered.

"How much water we got left?" he asked.

Looking in the containers, I told him, "'Bout half."

Feeling the ground, he said, "Hmm. Moist. We gotta be close to water. You go find it and fill those up."

I didn't want to leave him. Not just because he shouldn't be alone. I was afraid I wouldn't be able to find water or my way back. I said, "No. Gonna stay with you and help. You drink this." I handed the pouch to him.

"It ain't for drinking." Nodding his chin downward, "This thing gotta get clean. It infected."

"Jackson," I moaned. "What if I get lost?"

"Here," he handed me pieces of his shirt that he had used on his foot. "Leave yourself a trail.

"And..." I sucked in a big breath, "...what if there ain't no water?"

"Ground's wet. Feel it and keep moving till you find wetter and wetter ground. Bound to find water that way." He set his eyes on mine. "You can do it. Just be careful. Walk slow and listen for noises. Stay hid. 'Specially if you sense danger. I ain't in no rush and don't you be neither. I ain't going nowhere." Then he nodded. End of discussion. Mama did that all the time, too. I knew when it was time to do what I was told. So, I did.

I drained the water pouches, giving both of us a good swallow and using the rest to bathe Jackson's inflamed foot and ankle. Now I had no choice. We needed more water, and I had to find it.

Looking around our hiding place, taking in the landmarks of trees and growth, I grabbed our empty water containers and headed in the opposite direction to where we had already traveled. My heart was pounding in my ears and lurching into my throat. I was scared.

I was far enough into the forest that I felt completely alone. A near sound of dry leaves cracking made my legs go wobbly.

I stopped.

Wait.

Listen.

The noise grew louder.

I held my breath.

A relatively small, golden-brown animal carrying a branch from a bush scurried around a tree trunk. I let myself breathe. A little. Not completely convinced that the critter was the source of such a disturbance, I still didn't move.

Silence.

I took a few slow steps.

More rustling.

The Day I Saw the Hummingbird

It was more of those furry critters carrying pieces of plants, trees, and shrubs. And they were heading in the direction of what sounded like splashing. Sure enough, they led me to water.

Upon spotting me, one of them stood on its hind legs with its mouth full of twigs and with eyes wide open. I froze just like it did. The standoff ended when it must have decided I wasn't about to do it harm. It scurried off to join the others in making a dam across a narrow part of the stream.

With the bags filled to the brim with cool, fresh water and my thirst quenched, I hoped I would find my way back to Jackson. Would I see the trail I left or would the little rags have blown away or become covered? Or worse. Would a band of soldiers or a slave-hunting posse have found my trail, leaving Jackson and me exposed?

That was the day I started to pray. Having nothing—and no one—else to rely on, I turned to God. I didn't care if I was just talking to myself. Simply the idea of not being alone made me feel better. I wondered if that's how it started with Mama. Immediately upon seeing the first piece of cloth I'd left stuck to the undersurface of a prickly scrambling vine, I let out a sigh of relief. I collected it and the others I had left for my trail.

The Day I Saw the Hummingbird

When I arrived back to Jackson, I wanted to fall on my knees and hug him. Instead, I was taken aback by how sick he looked. The pink color on the lining of his eyes had faded to near white. It looked like Mama's tongue and the inside of her mouth the day she died. Jackson was panting and I could see his heart beating on his wrists, as fast as the wings of a hummingbird. There was that reminder again: a bird I once loved to see had become a harbinger of death. Apprehension soaked into me as I bent down to make contact with a semiconscious Jackson.

When I put a hand to his hot forehead, he stirred. Opening his eyes, he smiled at me. "Oscar," he panted. "You done made it."

I looked at his left leg. The swelling was now up to his knee, his skin covered in blisters oozing pus. How could this be? How could this happen so fast? I couldn't have left him for more than an hour. Only once before had I seen a wound that looked like this. It was at the plantation when one of the younger kids was out barefoot. That was one of the fortunate days the doctor made it out in time. The boy lost his leg and nearly bled to death. He was sick for weeks with an oozing stump and fever.

What am I gonna do? What am I gonna do!
Panicking, I couldn't think straight. "Jackson," I gently spoke in his ear.

"Hmm," he moaned.

The weakness in his voice made my heart sink. "Jackson," I risked speaking a little more forcibly. "We gotta move you."

Babbling something I couldn't make out, finally I heard him say, "You gotta go." He nodded his chin in what looked like the direction he wanted me to head. The direction we were going before we stopped.

My chest caved in on me at the thought of leaving him there to die. Overwhelmed with the dilemma, I couldn't move. But what if I stayed and he died, then what? "I dunno what to do," I said.

"You go." With every ounce of energy he had left, he raised his head and turned to face me. "You go. Get your freedom." Again, he nodded in what I felt was the direction he wanted me to head. "Lights," he whispered. "Not far," he moaned. Again, he said, "Lights," and fell back into a deep sleep.

Lights? What did he mean by lights? Overcome with grief and confusion, a fleeting memory moved through me of something Kitch had mentioned about lit lanterns.

I was too upset to remember with any clarity exactly what he had said. Not wanting to abandon my friend, I stayed by Jackson's side, crying until exhausted. Reality set in when a surge of wind rustled some trees. The motion, the sound, what dangers it could mean, brought me back.

Blinking away my tears, I stayed very quiet. Distress was still in my belly and I felt sick. I stayed by Jackson's side hoping he'd get better. Even if he didn't recover, I couldn't leave him to die alone. Not after all he'd done for me. I prayed to Mama to help us, figuring she was now next to God. I waited. It didn't take long before Jackson snorted a big gasping sound. It was his last.

Jackson was gone. My friend, my teacher, my protector died because he cared more about helping to free slaves than about being safe himself. He died bringing me to freedom. Freedom! Where was his freedom now? A fury rose in my belly that wanted to explode. Damn them all, every last man and woman who did this to him! I hated the South and everything it stood for more at that moment than I ever hated anything. And being scared to death alone in those woods only made my anger worse.

I pounded the ground next to Jackson's still-warm body. My breathing began to get heavy and loud, like a horse taking off on a gallop. No longer able to contain the surging emotions pushing at me from the inside out, I started to pace around Jackson's body. I must have worn a path around him an inch deep. The whole while, I was using every cuss word I knew, the ones I picked up from Prescott's foul mouth.

But it was when I set my eyes on the cane I made for Jackson that something split inside of me. I didn't know my heart could break any more than it had already broken when Mama had died. I was wrong. I swear, I *heard* my heart rip. It stopped me cold.

I marched over and took that cane in my trembling hands. Holding it high above my head, I let out a wail I can only imagine sounded like an animal being tortured and slammed that branch down over a rock.

CRACK! The thing split in two. One piece stayed in my clenched fists; the other flew into a nearby tree.

What happened next is hard to describe. First, there was a moment of dead silence, making all the ruckus that came before seem even louder. Then, a small bird screeched and flew out of the tree that was hit by the bottom half of the cane. I stood frozen with the broken cane in my still-tightened grasp, breathing like I had just run a mile. My mind became clear of everything but one thought: *that poor bird.*

I dropped the cane and sat on the rock, cradling my head in my hands. I knew I needed a good talking to, but there was no one but me to do it. No one to tell me to *hush now* or *shh.* I had given into my impulse to act out in anger. Someone in earshot could've heard me and that would've been the end of me. But the only thing I did was frighten a little bird—a scared little bird that flew away to somewhere safer. I knew then and there that I needed to be more like that bird, more like the settled-down person Mama and Jackson had tried to shape me into being so I could find my way to freedom.

I gently placed the cane on the ground near the rock and kneeled by Jackson. Tears and sweat ran down my face. I knew I had to leave him as he was. But before I left, I whispered in his ear, "I promise." I said out loud what I refused to say earlier when he asked me to promise to keep my head the next time I got the killing urge. "I love you, Jackson," I cried, "I swear, I do my best making you proud. Mama, too." I looked to the sky and asked Mama to please help me keep that promise.

Motivated by fear, I gathered my bag, a water container, and tore myself away from Jackson.

The Day I Saw the Hummingbird

* * *

For hours, I plowed through thick vegetation ignoring the hunger clawing my stomach. My blind determination paid off. I came to an opening in the forest. In the distance, there they were. Lights. Straight ahead was a small house. On each side of the front door were lanterns hung on hitches. They were shining brightly. I remembered what Kitch told me about lit lanterns being signals for safe houses. It was later I learned that darkened lanterns meant it was too dangerous to stop.

A middle-aged man greeted me. I was given a meal and food to take with me the next morning when I was told I had to go. I was also given a map of where the next stopping point would be.

I slept outside at the back of the house. I didn't care that I wasn't given a bed or tent. Out under the stars that night—the first time on my journey alone—I gave thanks for the lanterns, the safe haven, and for the bittersweet taste of freedom before I fell into an emotionally-drained deep sleep.

The Day I Saw the Hummingbird

Chapter Thirty-Three

The quiet call of life spoke to me as I set out the next morning. Mama's voice sang in my soul's ear as birds chirped their wake-up greeting. She kept telling me that I would be safe. A calmness wrapped itself around my young body and, just like that, my fear of death vanished. I was alive. I had made it this far. And I was determined to become another part of the forest, to lose myself among the trees, wildlife, rivers, and let the streams take me home to freedom. I had all I needed: clothing, shoes, some food, my knife, water, my dictionary, and the Bible. I also had gained firsthand experience on how to hunt and fish. And Jackson taught me how to follow moist ground to water. It was the first time I was on my own, but I felt prepared.

Although my heart ached for Jackson and so many before him, I was so glad to be alive. There was something about seeing those lanterns, their glow so bright it illuminated my weary soul. Those charitable and tolerant strangers who opened their door reminded me again that good people lived in this world. They helped me at great risk to themselves and for no reward. My heart warmed knowing that they wanted to help people like me, people different from them in almost every way but one: we are all human beings. And knowing that somehow lessened the big divide I felt between my people and those against us. It spoke to something more powerful than hatred. And it also spoke to something I felt was greater than just upbringing. Perhaps we are all made differently. Maybe some folks are born with a natural ability to put themselves in the minds and hearts of people who aren't the same as them. And other folks, well, they think their own little corner of the world is so special they don't care to look hardly past their own front door. And there are probably lots of people in between.

***

I had made it to the north of Alabama in safety and needed to rest before heading into Tennessee. The map my last host gave me showed that Tennessee had much less distance to cross than the earlier states I had already traveled. The next state I'd be heading into after

Tennessee would be Kentucky, a border state. There, I hoped help would be easier to find.

I was wrong.

I found out months later that, because Kentucky was one of the states that divided the South from the North, it was a *brother-fighting-brother* battleground. In 1861, a failed attempt by the Southern Alliance to gain control of Kentucky led to Kentucky declaring its allegiance to the Union. A lot of hostility from the South had roots there. Just because it was an abolitionist state did not mean it was a safe state.

But I didn't know any of this as I headed with confidence, courage, and optimism closer to the North. Had I known then what I found out months later, my newfound sense of calmness and faith in my safety would have most likely cracked. Maybe even crumbled like week-old cornbread.

As I had so many times before, I came upon a tributary (Jackson taught me that's what branches of rivers are called). Relieved it wasn't deep and surrounded by thick forest, I undressed and bathed. I was so proud of myself when I caught a fish with my hands the way Jackson taught me. A few minutes later, dried and dressed, I wasn't so lucky when I tried to start a fire. The wood was moist and wouldn't spark. And I had no luck rubbing stones together. I looked at that dead fish; its black eyes appeared alive, staring at me. My lips tightened in disgust. *That fish, he were alive till he met me. He just minding his business. And I done kill it!* But the shift of a single thought, *it food and my belly need it to keep going*, helped me feel a little better. I still had the queasy feeling, but I bit into the raw meat. The scaly skin was tough and hard to break with my teeth. When my attempt to eat it that way failed, I found a couple of large rocks. I gave it a pounding until its silvery scales cracked and the pink-beige flesh bulged through. I used my knife to scrape the meat away from the tiny bones. It tasted like the water it came from, fresh with a slightly salty aftertaste of algae. With my belly satisfied and my muscles weary to the bone, I laid my head on my bag, right on top of the books.

When I awoke to quiet, I was relieved that I had found a secure hiding place that had given me so much. Ready to set out again, I knew I should make it to the next safe house soon. My good fortune ran out when, after a few hours, I saw smoke ahead and heard the faint scream of voices in the distance. There were no gun sounds, but I couldn't be sure it wasn't fighting.

The Day I Saw the Hummingbird

Determined not to retreat back to where I'd come from, I had to find another safe spot and lie low. I took several timid steps, then listened. I repeated that until I felt satisfied that I wasn't in anyone's earshot who was waiting to pounce on me. As I moved along more rapidly, my heartbeat intensified, my breathing quickened, and I started to feel lightheaded. I opened my eyes as wide as they would go to keep from fainting. Finally, I had to stop and sit and wait for my body to calm down.

That's when I noticed something. Or nothing. The sounds I'd heard earlier were hardly there. I must have moved in the right direction. I took a slow breath through my nose and released a quiet, relieved sigh. I raised my eyes toward the stars, thanking whoever was watching out for me. I must've had some extra special help working day and night to keep me safe. How else did I make it this far?

Relieved by the feel of soggy ground, I knew I was, once again, close to water. The momentary relief I felt disappeared when I saw a skeleton on the path before me. Hairs bristled on the back of my neck. An itch that started on my scalp moved down to my arms. I wanted to turn away or run past it as fast as I could. But then my attention fixed on it. I couldn't help wondering if this had been a runaway that was tortured and killed like Sammy. Curiosity got the better of me. I crouched down for a closer look, trying to make as little noise as possible.

Never having seen a human skeleton before, my mind ran wild. Its small bone structure, not much longer than my height, made me think it could have been a child, a young girl or boy like me. I shivered when I thought about the color of his or her skin. A sinking sensation overcame me as I figured that this wasn't a white person left alone to die. No white child's body would be torn to pieces by vultures or other predators.

It scared me to think I may end up this way.

Then I got mad at myself for going off into these horrible thoughts. I'd witnessed so many terrible things before, and none of them had stopped me from going on. I had to move forward and that was that. I wanted to cover the bones, but (like before with Sammy and Jackson) I left it as I found it. I knew not to leave a trail back to me.

Once again, time had changed my mood. When I found what appeared to be another safe resting place in deep foliage, I settled in. I opened the package of food that was given to me before leaving my last stopover. Unfolding the corn cake seasoned with powdered sassafras leaves, I thought of Mama. She used to love to find clusters of saplings near the full-grown trees and dig up one or two. She'd cut the roots when they were full of sap and lay them somewhere cool and dark for a couple of weeks. When the flavor was ready for tasting, she'd add it to tea, rice, and soups. She sure knew how to spice things up with sassafras. Thinking about those pleasurable moments and the kindness that brought this meal to me helped me feel more settled. Having decided I was going to stay put for a while, maybe a day or two, I was glad the agitation in my body was gone.

The next two days were quiet; that was what I needed. I bathed in a watering hole, fished, observed nature, and slept. I picked up a smooth rock, similar to others I'd seen on river bottoms. The stones on the riverbed were different from those on the water's edge or on land, which were jagged and rough. I had time to wonder why. What effect did the water have stones? I was fascinated by the idea of how surroundings or temperature or even time of year shaped and influenced things as hard as rocks and as soft as little critters. Feeling the unwrinkled texture, I wanted to throw that river rock. It reminded me of my game with Sammy. I yearned for my friend. I yearned to play and feel carefree like we did those nights when Prescott left us alone and we enjoyed our time. I squeezed my fist around it and held back from making any motion for fear the noise could alert danger in my direction.

Yes, there were times I felt much older than I was. Mama called me an *old soul,* wiser than my years. But I didn't feel that way by the stream when I was thinking of playing with Sammy. I just wanted to be a kid and play. Feeling restless and not wanting to make a sound, I made up games to play inside my head. Then I remembered the books I'd been carrying this whole time. I could use this time to practice pronouncing words, but now I would do it silently. So, I pulled out Mrs. Whitfield's...my dictionary.

At first, I pronounced the alphabet in my imagination. It felt good. I could almost hear myself. Next, I opened the dictionary to any old page and silently pronounced a word. I started with short words, having no idea what they meant or how they sounded. The longer ones were real tricky, but I tried. *Maybe someday someone gonna help me with them fancy words.* I thought of words I knew—words that I liked and that made me feel good. And I thought of things said or I heard that made me feel bad. Just like noticing the difference with rocks—that river rocks are smoother than land rocks—I realized something important about all these words I was trying to learn. *They ain't just letters all tied up together. Words, they filled up with different meanings to different folk.*

Picking a word to test my idea, I decided upon *tree.* I silently spelled T-R-E-E. I looked at a tree near where I sat. It was then I realized how odd words are. T-R-E-E was not that thing my eyes rested upon. The word was not the thing. Words, I discovered were nothing more than groups of noises that were given meaning. But by whom? Who decided what to call a tree? And who decided that I was a Negro?

The Day I Saw the Hummingbird

Chapter Thirty-Four

I slept fitfully that night, not because of anything going on around me, but because it took a while for my new word game to end. I wanted to entertain myself, but what I had started was like a yawn or an itch that wouldn't stop. As fun as it was, it set my mind racing. The rest I needed didn't come easily. Regardless of my tiredness, when it was time to get up and go I continued to head north.

As I approached the place where I saw the smoke and heard the voices a few days earlier, I hesitated. Just being close to what felt like danger gave me the shakes. I asked for both strength and protection and, once again, I very slowly moved one foot in front of the other. I stopped every few minutes to listen and look around. Seeing nothing threatening and hearing no strange noises, I continued until I arrived at a burned-out campfire. It must have been the source of the smoke I saw days earlier. Particles of spat chewing tobacco were on the ground.

Tobacco. I heard those plantations were no better than the sugarcane plantations. Macy once told her papa, Albert, about the master being upset because his relatives lost crops in tobacco. They had to rent out some of their slaves to work on cotton and rice plantations to make up for their lost income. Macy was upset that families were split-up. Husbands were taken from their wives and children were ripped away at young ages. Mama used to tell me we were lucky to still be together because she had heard of boys as young as seven-years-old who had been separated from their parents.

Images struck my head: slaves laboring in the hot sun, sweat pouring off them like rain with barely a drop of water to drink or a small morsel of food to eat, toiling their entire lives away. And if that wasn't bad enough, there were despicable foremen (like Prescott) who tortured hardworking people just because they could or felt like it. My people were chained, hung, cut, whipped, raped. A delicate few were driven to madness. Women lost babies before, during, and after birth because of starvation. If they didn't die themselves, they had to go right back out into the fields. If they couldn't work, they were brutalized and some killed. And that's just what I either saw or heard about. If there was worse happening out there to people like me still on plantations, I didn't want to know.

Still looking at the wad of dried, chewed-up tobacco, my attention shifted to hoof marks in the dirt. Whoever they were, they left a trail going in a different direction than where I was heading. Not knowing where they came from, I hoped I wouldn't run into more of them on the way to my next stop. I had been lucky so far that I hadn't walked into any battles or skirmishes. Would my luck hold out?

The answer came when I arrived at the destination close to the Tennessee-Kentucky border, where an "X" was marked on my map, indicating a safe house. It was dark out, and no lights were on inside. There weren't lantern posts on the outside, so I tiptoed around to the back and found a barn. I carefully slid the big wooden door open and entered.

I heard a gasp followed by a cough.

I thought I was going to swallow my heart that was pounding so hard and fast in my throat. Afraid to make a move or do anything that could be heard, I froze. And waited.

There was some rustling overhead from a loft.

I didn't even dare back out of the barn.

Silence.

Finally, the tension broke when a man's voice said, "Who goes there?"

He didn't sound hostile. His tone reminded me of Kitch.

Silence. Was he waiting for me to answer? I wasn't about to fall into a trap after coming this far, so I kept quiet. Mama and Jackson would have been proud.

He repeated, "Who you are?"

I saw a leg come down a wooden rung on the ladder.

I wanted to run, but my feet felt stuck. I just stayed quiet.

When he came all the way down and stood before me, I let out a sigh that might have blown a small bird off course. He was a Negro like me.

One look and he patted my back. "Lemme help get you up there. Go on, now," he said grabbing hold of my bag.

Once atop, my attention went to a large opening in the siding that lit the wide space. By moonlight, I was led around the corner of piled horse food to their hiding place. In the small, protected space, I saw another man by the stack of hay who was wearing coveralls. The man who met me below said, "Mitchell here," as he reached a hand out to me.

His hand was smooth, and his clothes were neat—not ragtag, like mine. I knew that he wasn't a field slave. He must have been a conductor like Jackson. I smiled and gave his hand a thank-you squeeze and responded. "Oscar."

Mitchell then nodded to the scared-looking, large black man beside him. "This here be Russell. I be helping him."

Russell remained silent, but he spoke through big eyes that were surrounded by dark circles that held a ton of sorrow. He made his acquaintance with a single nod.

In front of them on a wooden box was a meal of thick soup and bread. Mitchell broke off a piece of his piece of bread and handed it to me. Russell did, too. They dipped their bread into the soup and encouraged me to do the same. No one had to tell me what to do or how to act. I knew to keep quiet. Jackson had taught me well. I stayed that way through the night, waking only to the sound of their coughs and snores.

When morning came and daylight flooded in through the opening, I got a better look at them. Russell's parched, cracked skin was covered in scabs, scars, and wounds that were in various stages of healing. His lips were dry and peeling, and the ridges surrounding his nose had a crusty yellow-brown film. His hands had callouses as thick as beetles, and his nails were chewed and splintered. He had bald patches on his scalp. It hurt my heart to see how beaten down he looked, and I wondered what his story was. Mitchell, on the other hand, smelled like fresh soap. He was clean with a short-cropped, full head of black hair. His light-brown, unblemished skin looked so, well, unspoiled, and he had hands and nails that didn't have hardly a speck of dirt on them.

"Good morning," Mitchell spoke in a low, barely audible tone.

I wanted to talk, to know more about them, where they were heading and, more importantly, if they were going north, could I join them. But before I could open my mouth, Russell stirred and caught my attention. He opened his watery, bloodshot eyes, looking like he'd been crying and hadn't had much sleep.

Mitchell put a hand on Russell's shoulder and gave it a compassionate pat then turned to me. "So, Oscar," he softly spoke, "where you be headed?"

Comforted that he addressed my concerns, I whispered back, "New York City." I thought of the note

Mrs. Whitfield had given me, the one I hoped I would deliver personally.

"That a long way up north." Mitchell was pensive as he stretched his neck to work out the tension his muscles must have held from sleeping on a hard surface. Finally, and to my relief, he asked, "Wanna come along with us? We going as far as Ohio. Connecting Russell here up with some folk there. I be coming back south after that." He then mentioned that people in Ohio could help me get where I was headed.

I wondered exactly where Ohio was in relationship to New York, but that didn't matter. I had a plan and someone to help me. Again. Without hesitation, I said, "Mighty kind of you to offer. Yeah, much obliged!" I looked to Russell, hoping for his approval.

Russell then spoke for the first time. "Come along, little man." He blinked away a couple of tears.

Overcome with appreciation, I sucked in a slow breath, looked into Russell's sad but kind eyes and said, "I sure do thank you."

Mitchell filled me in on the immediate plans, which were to wait for a meal, some food to take with us, and maybe a little money. He said that people offered what they could to help make a runaway's escape easier and hopefully more successful. Mitchell also told me that he knew the routes. He'd traveled them several times before as a conductor. He was another man working alongside a woman named Harriet. There was that name again. *Someday sure would love meeting you, Missus Harriet, and give my thanks.*

Before long, we heard someone approach the lower area. My muscles all seemed to tighten at the same time and didn't loosen up until a voice called out. "Food for ya'll."

Mitchell went down and, without mentioning my being present, he took the food and thanked the man for his hospitality.

I overheard mumbling.

When Mitchell returned, he had our morning meal and extra food to take with us. He divided the breakfast into threes and told us what was said. There was fighting surrounding where we'd be heading. "Listen up. No talking when we out there. Move slow and careful. You two stay behind me." He looked at me, then at Russell.

Feeling jumpy, I ate my portion of cornbread fast. Russell did, too.

Just before leaving, Mitchell boarded up the opening with its wood cover and straightened up the loft to make it look as if no one had been there. At his lead, we headed northeast, away from what I assumed to be the heaviest concentration of fighting near the Mississippi river. That decision was wise.

Well into Kentucky, we had some of the food given to us and bedded down. Before closing my eyes, I looked to the starry sky and asked for it to see me clear to my destination. The last thing I remember was a temporary streak of bright light flashing through the dense darkness. I wondered if that was a good sign.

The Day I Saw the Hummingbird

Chapter Thirty-Five

Guided by an experienced conductor who had already helped free several slaves (and by the grace of God), we made it close to Ohio. But I learned not to get too comfortable with plans. Or the sweet feeling of relief. One minute, everything seemed to be going just fine; the next, change shook everything up. It didn't take me long to learn that's not just life on the run, that's life.

It began with a cough. Russell didn't look well. Along the walk, he kept clearing his throat. When that turned into a barking "ahem," he brought up thick gunk. It started out clear, but within an hour the glop he was bringing up was dark greenish-brown. I had seen that before. I hoped he didn't fall ill like Mama had. But he was flushed with fever, and sweat dripped onto his parched lips. He took off the top layer of the shirt he was wearing. Every time he coughed, he looked around. I got pretty good at reading people's feelings from their faces, and Russell looked scared. Maybe he knew the sound he was making could give us away or maybe he knew he was sick. Either way, he was scared. I was, too.

The moment we stopped to rest in a brush-hidden area, Russell fell asleep. I was sure that would help him to feel better. I was wrong. Soon after I fell asleep, I was awakened by coughing fits of him wheezing and hacking in a panic.

It also woke up Mitchell, who rolled over and patted Russell's back to try to stop him from gasping to get air in. "Gimme a cool rag," he motioned to me. Then to Russell, "There, there now, calm that breathing." He slowed his words. "Real easy now."

Grabbing a piece of material, I wet it with our drinking water and handed it to Mitchell. He rubbed the rag over Russell's forehead. Mitchell shook his head. "He burning up."

Russell moaned, coughed up another big, thick brown blob and continued panting through pursed lips. For I don't know how long he continued to struggle to breathe. More gurgling sounds. Wheezes. When he fell backward, I knew he was in bad trouble. Just like Mama had been.

I could feel myself shutting down. It was too familiar, too similar to Mama's last moments. Just too much tragedy was piling up. A thundercloud of grief burst inside me when Russell let out a big loud gasp. Then nothing. Unable to control myself, I screamed, "No!"

Mitchell grabbed hold of me. "Shh, Oscar," he whispered in my ear. "Shh." As spray from his mouth hit my cheek, he held me like he was my papa. He held me like Jackson had.

I don't know how long it took, but I quieted down. Finally.

Silence.

Then sound.

Horses.

And screaming drunken voices bellowed, "We're gonna get them nigger lovers!"

Mitchell flattened my body flush with the ground, my face in the dirt. He held me down. Not resisting his attempt to keep us still, I cried into the dirt.

A couple more yells of unintelligible blather and laughter.

Laughter? That did it! I tried to wiggle loose from Mitchell's arms, but he was strong. And he was determined to keep us alive.

There it was again! I wanted to get up and lash out. Scream. Run to where they were and make them stop.

Would the urge ever go away? Then I remembered my promise to Jackson. I couldn't act up. I couldn't soil his memory by going against what he wished for me. And what Mama dreamed for me. But that didn't quiet my anger; it only kept me still.

I felt Mitchell's warm arm across my back, using all his might to keep me from moving.

Finally, Mitchell loosened his hold on me.

I looked up. Dust was still flying, but the screaming was gone. I hadn't realized it, but we were alone. Filled with raging anger remembering the laughter from those bastards, I erupted. "I hate them!"

"Hush you! You fixin' to get us killed!" His whisper was a stern as a preacher warning his flock about the evils of sinning, only a lot quieter.

No, I didn't want to get us killed. I didn't want Mitchell to get hurt. And, once again mindful of my promise, I bit my lower lip as he lifted his chin, listening to be sure we were really alone.

Holding up a hand, indicating for me to wait a minute, he peered out from the brush. "They gone." He looked at Russell's body. "Best move fast. Vultures. Sure sign…"

The few minutes it took for him to check for danger settled me. Wanting to make up for leaving Sammy and Jackson, "Can we set him in the ground? Not just leave him here." I pleaded.

"No time, Oscar. Gotta get a move on."

And we did. It was the way of the runaway to think of nothing but moving to the next safe place. Leave all else behind. What felt like a mountain pressed down on my body, making it hard to move and plow on to freedom.

I began to question the very notion of freedom. What was it? When this journey started, I thought freedom meant escaping Prescott and the horrors of plantation life. Kitch taught me another definition of freedom: opening my mind to be free to explore new words, ideas, and the worlds they could create. Then being free meant being hunted and existing with the guilt of the living and dead I left behind. Freedom, I was coming to understand was as complicated and confusing as life.

Feeling numb and empty, I followed behind Mitchell like a horse being walked the last mile of its climb up a hill, too tired to carry on.

Having lost all sense of how long we'd been walking, I took notice that the moon seemed to be moving toward the edge of the earth. I wanted to join it over the cliff and disappear. To not exist when the sun met the new day. When Mitchell scouted a relatively safe hiding place, we settled down to rest.

"Been a real rough one," he commented.

"Uh-huh," I moped.

"Hungry?" He motioned to what was left of our food supply, the last supper for three. I thought of that extra portion. Russell's share. Although my stomach was growling, I didn't want to eat. Feeling miserable, I shook my head *no*.

"Wanna talk?" he asked as he handed me my share.

I pushed it away and turned my back to him.

"Hard to see them things, Oscar." His voice cracked. "Trust me, I know." Although he never shared his personal history with me, I could tell by the way he responded that he'd been through his share of heartache.

There was something about his sorrowful low tone that got through to me. I wasn't the only one suffering. The gentleness of his manner moved me to open up. "I hate them drunken bastards. All they wants is to..." I stumbled to find the right word. "Own me. Control me. Treat me like I ain't a person."

Mitchell put a soft hand on mine. "Surely is truth in what you saying."

"You too, Mitchell. They wanna own you and all the rest of us, too. We just cattle to them. They even brand a man I knew. Why they do such a thing?"

"Ain't got no answers. But surely is terrible stuff. Terrible for folk to treat any other like that."

I looked at him, hot tears streaming from my eyes. Hostility seared through my body. I clenched my fists. Muscles in my back, limbs and torso tightened. "I hope every one of them die a slow, rotten death!" I pounded a fist in the dirt.

Mitchell grabbed hold of my shoulders. "Oscar," he held me, "you go on now and let it out. But hush when you do."

I broke from him, but he stayed by my side. Feeling him next to me, making room for what needed to come, I lowered my head to my hands and did let it out. Another torrent of crying gushed from my insides. And then anger resurfaced. Were it not for him, his decency and kindness—all he was doing to help me, and others—I might not have quieted down. Nothing was easy. Once again, I felt trapped by my own feelings that betrayed me over and over. Again I pounded the ground. When my hand slipped on a jagged rock edge, Mitchell jerked my body back around to look at him. Ignoring my bloody fingers, he refocused my attention on his face and in his frightened large black pupils that covered all the color in his eyes, I saw myself. The reflection I saw was of an angry child filled with hatred for one person I knew—Prescott—who caused me great pain. But the hate spread to everyone who represented that one real-life man. The *idea* of his kind was enough to set a rage burning in me that could easily go out of control. At that moment, I saw that I was no different than Prescott. We harbored the same hatred. And that scared me. It gave me pause.

Mitchell's voice echoed in the background. "Lemme get a wet cloth for your hand."

I wiped and wrapped my hand. I felt the searing pain I caused myself. I also felt Mitchell's full attention on me. I wanted to know, "Ain't you got hate for them?"

"Surely, I do. But I ain't gonna let it eat me. What earthly good would that do? It'd be like me putting my finger in a rattlesnake's mouth 'specting it to bite my enemy. I be the fool suffering poisoning. Carry hate and you gonna suffer worse. You gotta move on."

"No!" I protested. "No, I ain't gotta move on. I ain't never gonna forget all I seen! All that's happened! Never!"

Letting me purge, he kept whispering, "It gonna be fine. It gonna get better." He put his hand on mine.

After what felt like a long time, I began to relax and the anger faded. Then he really surprised me. He pointed to my bag and said, "I saw them books of yours. You wanna use them? You wanna learn? Why you got them if you ain't never gonna use them? You gotta move on. Find you a reason to live and stay alive. Them there books is a good reason as any."

I turned to look at him. Once again, there were his big, soft eyes. He got through to me, and what he said made a lot of sense. He sounded like my mama. I wiped my wet face and said to him, "You sure are smart."

"I dunno 'bout that," he smiled at me. "But lemme say this 'bout forgetting. You ain't never gonna forget. Best you can do is let go of what be causing you to suffer. Live life as good as you can. That ain't forgetting, Oscar, it be living."

What he said felt right; it sat comfortably in my belly. And feeling much better, I squeezed his hand. "Thank you for being my friend."

Again, he looked at me, his eyes deep and pained. "You a good boy, Oscar. I glad to be here with you." He glimpsed at the food. "How 'bout we eat now?"

The Day I Saw the Hummingbird

As we shared the meal, what he said earlier sunk in deeper. I learned a valuable lesson that day from Mitchell. Everything I'd experienced in my few years alive—and all my years to come—would forever be a part of me. They were my history, my memories. Feelings could be stirred up and return in waves like vomit. I just had to deal with it and move on. No sense spewing it around and messing up everything around me. The seeds of how to cope with all of it were planted, but I was still way too young to fully realize how to meet situations using my head and my heart rather than my gut reactions. After all, I was only just on the eve of turning ten years old.

Chapter Thirty-Six

The rest of the journey proceeded without danger. Finally, we made it to our destination in Ohio. Mitchell had told me that, from there, I would be given help to travel to New York City. As we arrived at a two-story house standing on a three-hundred-foot-high hill overlooking the Ohio River, he relayed more information to me. The owner of the home—Mr. John Rankin, a Presbyterian minister and educator—dedicated much of his life to the antislavery cause. His house had several secret rooms for hiding fugitive slaves. He left a light on in the front of the house to signal it was safe to approach. Mitchell told me that Rankin was a kind, generous man who kept slaves in his home until he got word it was safe to travel further north. He was among a sizeable group of Ohioans who risked their lives to help free slaves.

I didn't understand why Mitchell seemed so fidgety when we arrived in what I thought was a free state. He explained to me that, although slavery was not legal in

Ohio, the abolitionist movement was opposed by a lot of people living there because the residents feared that slaves would protest for equal rights and take jobs away from the white population. This proslavery movement in Ohio threatened the Underground Railroad. Mitchell then shared some of his own story about how he had been attacked and barely escaped a group of men attempting to stop the flow of fugitive slaves through Ohio. He also informed me that proslavery people were on the lookout for runaways so they could claim the reward for each captured and returned slave.

We were brought into one of the safe rooms, a comfortable space with two beds. Mr. Rankin appeared and sat with us. "We have a young one here." He smiled at me and held out a hand to shake. Receiving it, he then looked at Mitchell and released his grip. "Good to see you again, Mitchell."

"Same here, sir."

Without any small talk, Mr. Rankin continued on with Mitchell glancing in my direction every so often. "Things have heated up." Not understanding, I cocked my head. Mr. Rankin took notice.

Paying attention to the looks going on between Mr. Rankin and me, Mitchell smiled and said, "He a smart one." I figured it was an invitation to go ahead and talk freely in front of me. Mitchell proved me right when he went on to say, "This here boy seen a lot. He surely old for his age."

Mr. Rankin smiled and said, "Well then, I don't suppose I need to hold back."

"Don't reckon so, sir." Mitchell nodded.

Mr. Rankin then took on a very serious look. He had a lot of worry-wrinkles around his eyes and mouth, which got deeper the more he talked. "We've got some problems here. It seems that although the Northern States have passed laws making slavery illegal, there's still a whole slew of people honoring a Federal law passed many years earlier—way back in 1793."

Rankin liked to preach and give lots of details, which I found boring. Who cared what happened so long ago? I wished he'd just get on with the important part so I could rest. I wiggled my toes inside my shoes to burn off nervous energy and waited for him to get to the parts that concerned us and our plans.

My attention snapped to and he regained my interest when I heard him say something about a Fugitive Slave Law that guaranteed slave owners a legal right to reclaim their escaped slaves. Although I didn't fully understand everything he said, I think I got the gist of it. If I understood him correctly, the North wasn't safe for me, either. *What in tarnation?* All this traveling we'd done—all the danger we'd encountered—was on the wish and promise of freedom. Now I was hearing it might not really exist. Would I ever have a fair chance of living a life without bondage? Would I always live as someone seen and treated as less than a real person? Would the white man only see my skin color and not see me? Would I always wonder if anything I achieved as a freed slave could be taken away from me? Was that what life in the United States of America would always be like for Negroes?

Mitchell glimpsed over at me. Sweat bubbled on my upper lip, and I was rapidly tapping a finger on my thigh. He must have known that I felt unsettled. I wondered if it was as obvious to Mr. Rankin as he took his leave. Once he was out the door, Mitchell paced and rubbed the back of his neck.

All the talk about Fugitive Slave Laws had me jumpy enough. When Mitchell got quiet, I became more nervous. Was he thinking of backing out of his promise to help me get to New York City?

Before my mind could take me too far into that briar patch, Mitchell turned to me and spoke. "I reckon a trip to New York City would surely do me some good."

Did I hear him right? "What you say—"

"You been done wrong lots, Oscar." He came to me and patted my back. " You ain't gonna go thinking yourself into a bad state, is you? They lots a good people out there helping. Here on out, it gonna be easier. I promise you that."

I knew that his promise was just to make me feel better. Who could possibly guarantee such a thing? But it did help me relax. "Thank you," I sighed in relief. Maybe it was my reward for keeping my promise to Jackson. Confirmation that it *was* the right choice.

"Yeah, it'll do me good to see you clear to New York City."

The decision was made, but we wouldn't be safe to leave for over a couple of months when the unrest Mr. Rankin told us about settled down. We remained past my tenth birthday, which we celebrated with a delicious spice cake. For our safety, we never ventured beyond our room or the privies room. Therefore, I had no idea if Mr. Rankin had a wife or family. I assumed his cook made the cake.

The Day I Saw the Hummingbird

While we were there, Mr. Rankin learned that I had started to read and write. Being another kind soul, he arranged to have a friend come over to help me with lessons. "I have many friends who want to assist, and I know just the person to come and work with you," he said.

While Mitchell busied himself helping with odd jobs in our room (like polishing silver or shoes and fixing damaged objects with glue like pottery or small pieces of furniture), I had help from Miss Pritchfield, a retired schoolteacher. She was happy to be of service to the minister in his work with escaped slaves. Building on what I had already learned, she taught me about diction and the proper use of nouns and verbs. I spoke words I had never heard before. To help me learn their meanings, she had me break words into parts so I could understand where they came from. It amazed me that some English words went back to other languages like Latin and Greek. She was patient and answered all my questions. She encouraged me to keep at it and even suggested that, when I arrived wherever I was ultimately going, I try to further my studies. This elderly, gray-haired white woman with tiny arms, a small waist, and a short, bent stature filled me with excitement, confidence, and a hunger to learn more than ever.

"Reading and writing will open doors for you, Oscar," she'd say many times as her wrinkled skin smoothed with her smile.

There was that use of *doors* once again, but this time I understood what she meant. "Yes, ma'am."

"You're a bright young man. One of the smartest I've worked with," she patted my hand.

Her pale skin upon my dark skin was a vision that made me feel warm inside. I'd never been around an elderly white woman like her, and it opened up feelings in me that I'd carry for the rest of my life. "Thank you, ma'am," I'd respond over and over, feeling so filled with pride.

When it came time for Mitchell and me to leave, I felt sad saying goodbye to Miss Pritchfield. I had grown quite fond of her. The last time I saw her, she told me, "You've learned to use that dictionary of yours. Continue looking up new words and the next time I see you, your vocabulary will exceed mine." Then she gave me one of her sweet smiles, but this one had a touch of sadness in it. I think we both knew there wouldn't be a next time. Just like with Mrs. Whitfield, I will never forget Miss

Pritchfield's kindness or the door she opened that boosted my self-confidence.

***

With the farewells behind us, the next stage of my travels with Mitchell began. We were put in a box and stored under hay on a horse-drawn wagon. Although easier than walking through unknown terrain and hiding behind bushes, I still felt like an easy, defenseless target. I held tight to myself every day and enjoyed getting out at night at the safe houses. When the bumpy, multi-day journey finally came to a stop, I got out to stretch my legs. I was completely surprised by what I saw.

It was a boat.

I looked to Mitchell, who was having a laugh at my reaction. "You ain't never seen a boat before?"

"No," I replied. "Where we be?"

"Lake Erie. That boat gonna get us to New York."

"Really? We almost there? New York City?" My voice was high, like a little child who was excited to get something sweet for being extra good.

Mitchell grinned but shook his head. "No, Oscar. New York. The state. And a big one. Bigger than

Louisiana, Mississippi, and even Ohio. We got us a far piece to go till we get us to New York City. And that be after we set foot on dry land."

"Oh." My voice returned to normal. "Well, we still closer than before."

"You betcha."

Unlike big slave ships from Africa that my mama and Albert used to talk about from stories they'd heard, this boat was different. It looked like a little wooden house. It had big square windows on the sides and a place to sit up top. We'd be down below, out of sight. As soon as we got on board, I felt strange. My balance was off and my belly kept flip-flopping. That didn't let up for the days we were traveling in cold weather and rough waters. We were fed, but I had a mighty hard time keeping food down. When we docked in Buffalo, New York, I must've been five pounds lighter. My clothes were baggy on me. I was sure glad to leave that part of the trip behind.

From there, we traveled over land to the address that was on the envelope Mrs. Whitfield had given me. Moving through backwoods, we arrived at a city that had more buildings, people, horses and moving carts in it than I ever saw in one place. Even with all the commotion, I was scared that I'd be spotted and shipped back to

Louisiana. It was a relief to finally arrive at the Whitfield's doorstep in New York City. They lived in a nice-sized house just outside of the main city.

We were met at the door by a pleasant-appearing couple. We made our introductions. Terrance Whitfield looked like his brother, Maxwell, with less forehead hair but every bit as calm and quiet in manner. His wife, Jane, had a pleasant smile. She was a short-statured, slim woman with long brown hair. The hug she gave me made me feel welcome from the very beginning. She was equally kind to Mitchell.

She put a hand on my arm and said, "Won't you two come on in?" I found out later that somehow Sarah Whitfield had gotten word to them that I'd be coming.

We followed them into what she called "a drawing room" where she motioned for us to have a seat on the couch. My clothes were dirty, and I felt embarrassed. I didn't want to sit down. Mitchell didn't either. He said, "Don't wanna dirty—"

"Oh, nonsense, sit," She smiled as we sat. Her husband also nodded a smile.

Before anyone said anything else, I reached into my bag and pulled out the dictionary. In it was the neatly sealed envelope that I was to give to them.

The missus' eyes were on the dictionary and the letter in my hands. "Did you have something you wanted us to see?" she asked.

"Yes, ma'am." I stood and walked slowly to the couch where they were seated. Lowering my head, I handed the sealed note to her. I heard her shuffle the pages and sniff as I walked back to where I was sitting and took my seat. She pulled a handkerchief from the sleeve of her dress and wiped tears forming in her eyes. When she finished reading the letter, she was full-out crying. She wiped her chin and handed what she'd just read to her husband.

Mitchell and I sat silently waiting, not understanding why she was crying and why her husband was also tearing up. When Mr. Whitfield finished studying the pages, he looked at me with soft, watery eyes. "That dictionary, that's a present from my sister-in-law?"

Holding it between my hands, I said, "Yes, sir."

"Oh, my boy," he shook his head and let out a big sigh. "That dictionary is a very special book." He seemed overcome with some feeling I couldn't name and stopped talking.

Jane Whitfield continued. "Oscar, what my husband is trying to say to you is that my sister-in-law gave you a dictionary that she bought for her son, Zachary." She then surprised me when she got up and came to sit by me. Putting a hand on top of mine, still on the dictionary, she cleared her throat and continued through an unsteady voice. "Her son died…"

While the missus attempted to find her composure, Mr. Whitfield added, "From a horse accident. Nobody's fault. It bucked, and he fell off. The good lad hit his head."

"We wanted you to know that," added the missus, "she hasn't been able to part with any of his things until this." She went on to tell us that Zachary Whitfield was eight-years-old when he died. His death happened several months before I arrived. Sarah Whitfield, unable to bear her son's death, created a kind of holy place in their home that held all of her son's earthly possessions. Maybe she thought that having his things around her was the next best thing to having him with her. "She sent me a letter that preceded you here," Jane Whitfield paused. "She said you reminded her of her son. Not in appearance but in how her heart felt about you. She said she hoped you would show up at our door someday. And here you are. We had no idea about that dictionary."

I choked out the words, "Sorry hearing 'bout her boy. She so good to me." I patted the dictionary. "She help me plenty in learning with this. Save me many a time, her lessons, times when it were hard to keep going on." Looking at Mitchell who now had a smile as wide as a bridge across the Mississippi River, I added, "I ain't never gonna forget her kindness." *That be why Mrs. Sarah Whitfield so awful sad when she tended me.*

"Well, Oscar, clearly our sister-in-law was taken with you," the mister said.

To that the missus added, "She wanted you to stay here with us and give you a job as our houseboy—"

"Oh, my." I didn't mean to interrupt her; it just popped out.

"That's not all." She stopped. Looking at her husband, who nodded, she continued. "She wants us to carry on with your learning. She told you we're teachers?"

Too beside myself to know what to say, I responded, "Yes, ma'am," once again.

"Well, Oscar, we could use help around the house. But I'm afraid there's not enough work for it to be full-time."

Just when I thought the bad news was coming, she grinned her pearly-white teeth right at me. "So, that would give you extra time to study. How does that sound to you, Oscar?"

Before I could open my mouth to respond, we were all in tears.

* * *

Mitchell stayed on with us for a few days to help me settle in and to rest from all his exhausting traveling. He also met with people he'd be working with to help free more slaves.

Thus began my new life, one that would see me through to many happy, fulfilling years of working for the Whitfields. I started as a houseboy, doing odd jobs. Later, I was promoted to Butler. Even though they employed me, they treated me like family. Two years after I arrived, they had a baby girl, Emelia. She became another unexpected and joyful part of my life along with tending to her kind, generous parents. And I always had plenty of time to study, read, write, ponder, and wonder. My curiosity never faded and my love for learning only intensified. I even taught Emelia a thing or two.

At night before I go to sleep, I read passages from the first book I owned, the Bible. And I look out of my bedroom window to the stars above and tell my mama, "I'm fine. I'm free."

The Day I Saw the Hummingbird

EPILOGUE

Summer 1914

That was a long time ago, my escape, and so much has happened since. I never imagined I'd return to the South, not after all the sorrowful memories and nightmares I'd left behind fifty-two years ago. Although I felt excitement over hearing Booker T. Washington's lecture, I also felt unsettled, like a man who didn't belong. Why? Well, for the few years I lived in the South as a young slave, I didn't belong—as a valued human being. My years in the North changed that; and through loving kindness, being accepted into a household where I was treated like family, I gained the sense of belonging I had yearned for since my mama's death.

Did my time living with the Whitfields in New York City make up for all my childhood suffering? I'd like to think it did. They gave me so much: a home, work, education, and friendship. I loved them. There were so many good friends along the way, but being back in the South, so close to where it all started, gave me pause.

I never married. Being with the New York Whitfields felt like family enough. But I often wonder if the real reason I never got close to anyone in *that way* was the pain that lived deep in my heart. The wounds that never heal rise up when I see someone hurting. Or when I read about an injustice. Or, like today, when I saw a black woman bowing her head in submissiveness to a white man. I can't escape the reminders. There are too many. But despite all the injury, my soul holds immense gratitude that washes over me like the waves of the Atlantic Ocean, bringing me back to solid ground.

Through the years, I've learned a lot from books. But I still believe that my experiences with kindhearted people were my best education. Those were the inspiring lessons that lifted me up. The deceased Mr. and Mrs. Whitfield from Mississippi, now in heaven with their son Zachary, Kitch, Jackson, Mitchell and so many others who helped me—bless them all. From these good folks, I learned about a different kind of freedom. I thought I had to get out of the South, escape the plantation, to be free. I came to understand that freedom wasn't just escaping the chains, guns, dogs, and oppressive laws—the institutional barriers that existed for me and people like me. And still do to this day. No! My personal freedom came from inside of me when I realized that, no matter where I am, my thoughts and feelings are the invisible chains shackling me, the master enslaving me. My attitudes shaped my life. And life is too short to harbor bitterness. There is too much to be grateful for to burn daylight on resentment. That was the realization that set me free. Little did I know so many years ago that when my mama encouraged me to flee with Sammy, she wasn't just freeing me from bondage, she had (once again) given me the gift of life.

Taking my seat in that big assembly hall, I remembered the last time I was in Alabama traveling with Jackson. I also thought of the last time I saw Kitch, Macy, and Albert. What happened to all of them? I guess I'll never find out. Perhaps that's a good thing.

Smiling, I thought of the woman who would be honored today, the mysterious, heroic woman named Harriet: Harriet Tubman. After dedicating her life to helping free countless slaves, she died a year ago at the age of ninety. My smile widened as I also thought about the man who would be speaking: Booker T. Washington. He had done so much to help see Negroes enter schools. *Maybe I'll have a chance to meet him face-to-face. If I do, I'll tell him that I'm one of the lucky ones who learned to read and write.*

After the lecture, I would head back to New York City to be close to the aging and frail Whitfields. I wanted to continue to return the help they so freely gave to me.

POST NOTE

The Underground Railroad, a system of connections of secret routes and secure houses in the United States, was established to help slaves escape to free states and Canada. It was a network of abolitionists and friends, black and white, free and subjugated, which assisted the runaways. It was allegorically named "underground" because it was a secret, hidden resistance movement. It consisted of places to meet, clandestine routes, transportation, and safe houses. Anti-slavery sympathizers, church leaders, and congregations provided assistance. Conductors came from differing backgrounds, including white abolitionists, free-born blacks, and former escaped or manumitted slaves. Although some traveled by boat, train, or wagon, the majority went by foot. Due to the risk of discovery, information was mostly passed along orally. Fugitives were not the only ones at risk; many free blacks were often kidnapped and sold into slavery. Where money was to be made, freedom was fragile.

The Day I Saw the Hummingbird

When clashes between the North and South escalated in the Civil War, many blacks—slaves and freed—fought for the Union Army. After the end of the Civil War, in December 1865, the Thirteenth Amendment to the Constitution, which outlawed slavery, was ratified.

ABOUT THE AUTHOR

Paulette Mahurin lives with her husband, Terry, and two dogs, Max and Bella, in Ventura County, California. She grew up in West Los Angeles and attended UCLA, where she received a Master of Science Degree.

www.ingramcontent.com/pod-product-compliance
Lightning Source LLC
Chambersburg PA
CBHW060353260626
47160CB00006B/2291